To Debbie —
Hope you enjoy the book!
Cheri Winkivine
2012

QUICK KILL

Cheri Wickwire

Order this book online at www.trafford.com
or email orders@trafford.com

Most Trafford titles are also available at major online book retailers.

Printed in the United States of America.

ISBN: 978-1-4669-6022-0 (sc)
ISBN: 978-1-4669-6023-7 (hc)
ISBN: 978-1-4669-6024-4 (e)

Library of Congress Control Number: 2012917686

Trafford rev. 10/15/2012

 www.trafford.com

North America & international
toll-free: 1 888 232 4444 (USA & Canada)
phone: 250 383 6864 ♦ fax: 812 355 4082

CHAPTER ONE

I t is what it is and it was what it was. That's an Old Irish saying that her grandmother used to say. That's precisely what Quinn was thinking as she continued to pack clothes into her suitcase. Quinn had been waiting anxiously for this day to arrive. Two months to rest and do whatever she pleased. In a few hours she would be in the air and free of all the worries and pressures she had endured for the past three months.

Quinn Sonora Reaghan was a United States Federal Prosecutor. She had completed law school at UCLA, served an internship for a Federal Judge in Washington, D.C., and is now happily residing in sunny San Diego.

Her last case had taken months of work, researching, pretrial motions, jury selection, and finally the trial. The defendant had been sentenced to life in prison.

Quinn had felt remorse for the defendant's parents. They faithfully attended the proceedings everyday. The defendant was their only child. At the end they must have accepted the fact that their son was going to be found guilty of murdering his wife on their honeymoon. The evidence clearly showed he was guilty. They resided in Florida. It must have cost them a fortune to travel to California and stay for the six-week trial.

The Mother always wore a suit and a different hat every day.

The couple sat quietly during the trial, sadly watching their only son being accused and convicted of a heinous crime.

Quinn felt badly for them but not for their son. He had murdered his young wife while on a Mexican cruise. He had strangled his wife during a meaningless quarrel. He thought he had killed her. He panicked and threw her body over the railing into the swirling waters below. He thought he had killed her but she was only unconscious. She had died as a result of drowning, not from strangulation. He had panicked again when he came upon a ship's employee and in his fear and guilt shouted that because of the harsh winds his wife had fallen overboard.

The ship's captain was notified and immediately ordered the ship turned around to begin a search. The coast guard joined the search and within hours her body was found, floating on top of the water. The interesting thing about the body was the back of an earring was still attached to her ear lobe.

The husband claimed there were two Israeli Mossad agents on board who were after him for writing negative comments about his treatment in Israel on a recent trip. He contended they had killed his wife as revenge. There were two Israeli men on the passenger list. They were registered as wedding photographers. They did testify during the trial. The jury believed them and not the defendant. He was convicted of murder within a day of deliberating.

Quinn thought the jury was extremely conscientious. They listened intently and were well aware of everything going on in the courtroom. It wasn't always easy to select a well-rounded jury. The process took over a week because over three hundred jurors were summoned.

Each candidate had to fill out a three-page questionnaire. It was a lengthy process but an important one. The jurors came from many miles away from the Federal District Court in downtown Los Angeles. They were scheduled to serve in the district court three months. They could be called to serve on juries for several cases during that time.

This particular case the press nicknamed, "The Honeymoon Cruise Murder." The jurors got to tour the cruise ship and many of them enjoyed the experience of sitting on a jury that made national news.

Now it was over and Quinn could take a much deserved vacation. Her flight was leaving Lindberg Field in just a few hours so she was hurrying to get packed and ready the house for her time away.

The shuttle to the airport was picking her up and delivering her right to the door of the terminal.

Once she was on her way, she was free of anymore hassles until she arrived at the airport.

Quinn heard the beep of the shuttle bus just as she was picking up her purse and laptop. She grabbed her Kindle Fire from her nightstand and threw it into her purse, clutched her suitcase, and wheeled it to the curb. Her long awaited vacation was about to begin.

The shuttle bus picked up a few additional passengers before continuing on to the San Diego Airport. The bus was approaching the Harbor Drive intersection when Quinn looked out her window and saw a cruise ship sitting in the harbor-awaiting passengers to embark on a cruise. She wondered if it was the same ship as the one in her case but noticed the name displayed on the ship cruise line was entirely different.

The case had made headlines worldwide. CNN and FOX News had all sent reporters to the trial. It made her wonder if future cruise passengers, especially those on their honeymoon, had hesitated, just for a brief moment, of their destiny before boarding the ship.

CHAPTER TWO

Quinn was married but not living with her husband. She had met her husband while going to law school. Brixton Axlerod Rainwater had been a graduate student in law school. He was presently a member of the LAPD. He was drop dead gorgeous and arrogant as hell. She had not wanted a serious relationship with anyone and was certainly not looking for a man at that point in her life. As luck would have it, she instantly fell head over heels in love.

Brick, as his friends called him, was a product of two very unlikely parents. His father, Jack Rainwater, was a famous stuntman for several studios in Los Angeles. His mother, Jane Emerald Brixton, was a socialite from San Francisco. His grandfather was in the state legislature and a very well-known attorney in the Bay area.

Quinn and Brick dated for six months before impetuously deciding to get married. This happened before either of them had made plans which direction to go after graduation. It turned out Brick stayed with the police department and Quinn went to Washington, D.C., for a year.

They had an apartment in Los Angeles and she had a small apartment in D.C. The commute was difficult but they both had careers to pursue and they tried hard to make it work. Quinn would fly to California every other weekend and Brick would fly to D.C. whenever he didn't have duty on the other weekends or during the week.

The problem with the marriage began when Brick began auditioning for parts in movies and commercials. He already had an "in" with his father already in the business. He knew a lot of people in the studios and with his good looks he was a natural new talent.

Quinn loved him and put up with his being gone on location and going to all the hoopla and parties when she was home. She came home to spend time with him and to rest from her busy and hectic job. The routine had begun to wear on her and consequently on their marriage.

Brick was promoted to detective within two years. Quinn thought that would slow his extracurricular activities and it did for awhile. He loved the police force. He was a good officer and was highly regarded by his superiors.

After completing her internship, Quinn accepted a job with the government as a federal prosecutor. She moved back to Los Angeles and she and Brick bought a home in Redondo Beach. They both loved the ocean.

They discussed beginning a family but decided to wait until Quinn was sure she was ready to quit her job and settle down. She was sure she didn't want to have a child only to place them in someone else's care.

Brick couldn't stay away from the movies. He became very popular and soon had his own fan club. The police department used him to promote public relations. He had the best of both worlds.

Quinn was finally tired of the constant arguments and his absence from home. They tried to work it out but finally she had enough and moved to San Diego. It took sometime to reach a compromise but now they were friends.

They saw each other several times a year and she was always present when a new film premiered. They shared assets and they always filed their taxes as a couple.

Holidays were spent together with their parents, either in California or New York. Their parents thought they were a very strange couple but they didn't interfere. In their opinion, this new generation was a bit odd anyway.

Quinn and Brick knew eventually they had to make a decision about their relationship but for now it was easier just to play the game and continue with their separate careers.

Maybe in time that would change but for now it was working out just fine.

CHAPTER THREE

Quinn settled back into her seat on the plane and waited for the flight attendant to close the doors and begin the announcements and prepare for takeoff.

Quinn always sat in the emergency row. It was more comfortable with her long legs. She was five feet nine and she needed the extra space. Plus she had the assurance no mothers with small children would be in the seat next to her. She loved children but she liked to work while flying and preferred not being interrupted.

The flight would take about six hours. She had a layover in Chicago for an hour but then the flight to Buffalo would be short. She had arranged for a rental car. The drive to her parent's home would just be a little over an hour.

She checked her cell phone to make sure it was off and closed her laptop and leaned back to enjoy the view of San Diego disappearing from the horizon.

It was time to think of going home and spending time with family and friends. She looked forward to attending her tenth high school alumni, which was happening while she was there. Going home to a small town meant many reunions and fun times.

Quinn exited the plane in Buffalo and followed the arrows to Baggage Claim. She anxiously waited for the carousel to circle once she spotted her luggage fall from the chute. She had grabbed her suitcase and was just depositing it on the ground when her arm was suddenly grabbed. Turning around she was pulled into a hug and kissed on both cheeks.

"Mom," she exclaimed, after seeing her mother, once she was let go. "What are you doing here? I told you I had rented a car. Is Dad here too?"

"Yes, dear, he went to park and he should be here any minute. We thought it was crazy to have you rent a car when we still have your jeep at home. No one ever drives it except your dad once in awhile just to keep the engine in working order. So we just hopped in the car and came to pick you up. How was your flight?"

"The trip was fine. No problems. I am so happy to see you!" Quinn gave her mom another hug and broke away to turn and give her dad one too. "It's so great to see you, dad. This is a wonderful surprise. To tell the truth, I wasn't looking forward to making the drive to Grey Falls River after such a long day traveling."

"We'll stop for dinner on the way home," said her dad. "Then we can relax once we get there."

Grey Falls River, New York, was a small town in the northwest corner of the state. It was a community of small lakes and dense forests. Fishing and hunting were the primary activities of its citizens.

Quinn enjoyed the beautiful views as they rode along the highway. Everything looked the same but she was never tired of the lush green countryside and the smell of the pines.

Her parent's house was a gorgeous old, three story victorian with gables and gingerbread trim. It was painted a lovely yellow and had black shutters and black ironwork fencing surrounding the property.

When Quinn was in college her dad finished off the apartment above the garage for her to live in. It gave her privacy and a quiet place to study and entertain friends.

Her parents assured her it had been cleaned and repainted and was ready for her visit. This was welcome news. Quinn couldn't wait to settle in and relax in her old place.

Turning into the driveway was a dream come true after all those tough months of work. She was home at last.

Gathering her luggage, she followed her parents up the stairs to her apartment. She promised to join them for dessert after she unpacked.

Quinn simply collapsed in her chair after her parents left the apartment. She didn't even want to move a muscle. She closed her eyes and began to relax . . . just for a few minutes, she thought.

The ringing of her cell phone jarred her out of a deep slumber. She was startled to see her watch reading almost an hour later. She assured her mother she would be right down to share in the dessert her mom had prepared just for her.

It was over two hours later that Quinn finally came through the door to her garage apartment, determined to stay put for at least the next twelve hours.

Emptying her suitcases went smoothly. She placed all her cosmetics and personal items in the bathroom. Her robe and nightie and slippers were all placed neatly on her bed. As she slowly undressed, she thought to herself that it was great to be home. It had been too long.

CHAPTER FOUR

The next morning Quinn decided to take the jeep out for a spin around town. Maybe she would run into some old friends and find someone to have lunch with.

The streets of the old town were bordered on either side with large maple trees. The main street of town was only a few blocks long. Railroad tracks divided the shopping area from the part of town, which housed the bars and old hotels. Many years ago when the town was built, the lumber and oil companies had employed mostly men who quickly established places for their after hours pleasure. There were fewer bars now but the town was still divided by the railroad tracks.

At one time Grey Falls River had over twenty large manufacturing companies in town. That number had fallen greatly due to the recession in recent years.

The economy had suffered and many businesses had closed their doors or moved elsewhere.

Quinn was pleased to see the old but stately white pillars of the Elks Lodge gracing the large brick building in the center of town. She had spent many happy hours there as a child. Her uncles and grandfather had taken her there for lunch occasionally. Today both her parents were members and quite involved in the different Lodge activities.

"Oh my gosh," thought Quinn as she spotted the old town library. "It's a restaurant! When did that happen? And where is the Sears store that sat on the corner? The bakery is a Chinese restaurant? Have I been gone that long?" she mused.

The Grey Falls River Gazette building came into view as Quinn turned the next corner. She decided to stop there and see if an old friend from school still worked there. The building was old but still looked formidable as she parked and got out and climbed the old steps up to the heavy entrance door.

The first thing she noticed as she entered the building was the smell of newsprint. "At least that hasn't changed," she murmured to herself.

The reception area was still a high counter with a desk area behind it. High windows graced the sides of the room and ceiling fans slowly whirled above the room. A young woman approached the counter and asked if she could help Quinn with something.

"I'm looking for an old friend. Her name is Penny Stovall. She used to be a reporter here."

"Of course," the young woman replied. "Come with me and we'll see if she's busy. I know she will be delighted to see an old friend."

Quinn followed her down the hallway until she paused at an open doorway. She motioned Quinn to follow her into the room. There, behind a large desk, sat her friend, Penny, typing away on a computer, a serious look on

19

her face, totally absorbed in what she was typing.

"Excuse me, Penny, but you have a visitor. I could have paged you but I thought a surprise would be more fun," said the girl.

"Oh my word," Penny exclaimed as she jumped from her seat, knocking the chair backward. You have got to be kidding me! Is it really you, Quinn Reaghan?"

Quinn eagerly ran to her friend and enveloped her in a hug. "Yes, it's me, in the flesh! I'm home for a visit and I just couldn't wait to see if my old buddy was still slaving away at being the town's best reporter! How are you, Penny? You look fantastic!"

"Well, so do you, Q!" Hearing her old pet name made Quinn smile even more.

"Can you break and go to lunch with me?" asked Quinn.

"You bet I can," Penny replied. "Let's get out of here and go do some catching up!"

Penny was surprised to see the old jeep sitting in the parking lot. "I can't believe you still have that jeep! We had some great times in that baby! This is just unbelievable! I feel as though I'm dreaming! When did you get here and how long are you staying? Are you going to the alumni? Is Brick coming too?"

"Whoa, slow down, Penny! Your questions are flying too fast!" Quinn smiled at her friend and paused for a moment to pull into the parking lot of the local diner. She shut off the car engine and leaned back against the seat.

"Where to begin . . . It has been a long time. I flew in yesterday. I'm alone. Brick and I have different ideas about what we want in life so at the moment we are living apart. I still love him deeply but at the moment our careers are keeping us at a distance. As for the alumni, yes I will be attending. I will be happy to help with anything that needs to be done."

"I am so sorry about your problems with Brick, Q. I hope it works out for both of you. You're both terrific people and I know you can make the right decision, just give it some time." Penny patted her friend's hand and gave it a brief squeeze.

21

"Let's go have some lunch," Quinn exclaimed as she grabbed her purse and opened her door. "I'm starving for some home cooked food. I want to hear all about your family and what's going on in town. Fill me in on the alumni and bicentennial plans too. I am ready to relax and see what small town America is like once again!"

While they were eating their lunch, Penny told Quinn that she had been divorced for four years. She was now dating one of the firemen in town. She had a five-year-old daughter and he had a three-year-old son.

Quinn thought that was a wonderful story and was very happy for her friend. Her first husband had been in the service. He left for overseas as a good man but when he came back he became abusive and hard. Penny said being in a war zone scarred him. They were still friends but the relationship just would never work again.

Quinn asked her who provided childcare when she worked. Penny said her mother watched her daughter on days she didn't go to school.

The friends continued to chat until the meal ended and Penny had to return to work.

Quinn was thrilled she had made contact with one of her best friends. She promised to call her soon and make plans to go shopping or just have an evening together.

The afternoon was still young so Quinn drove by her old high school and then checked out the old haunts where she used to go on dates. Some were no longer there. One was just a parking lot. The old movie theater was now an office building. Now that was a disappointment. It had always been old. The red velvet seats had been worn thin when she was a girl. The ornate scrollwork had been something to see. The place always smelled of popcorn. Quinn smiled when she thought of some of the dates who had taken her there. She wondered what they were doing now.

CHAPTER FIVE

The day had begun with blue skies and warm sunshine but by the time she decided to head home, the sky was gray and the temperature had dropped a few degrees. Quinn was excited about the prospect of a thunderstorm. California did not have the kind of weather that was common in the eastern part of the United States. Crashing thunder and terrifying lightning streaks that lit up the sky and pouring rain that pelted the ground with heart stopping intensity.

Quinn drove to the far side of town where the local cemetery was located. It was quiet and peaceful there. Tall maples dominated the site. The older section had tombstones, a few mausoleums, and many statues and memorials standing as a tribute to the fallen heroes of Grey Falls River soldiers.

Quinn drove on to the newer section of the cemetery. A plaque lying flat marked the graves in this section embedded in the ground. It was beside one of these graves that Quinn knelt and placed a rose she had picked from her mother's garden that morning.

The plaque read: Quade Mervin Reaghan

1935-1984

Quinn gently placed her hand on the stone and traced the lettering before rising to her feet and getting back into the jeep. A few tears escaped her eyes and flowed down her cheeks. She was surprised by the emotion she was feeling. She had never known this man who had been lying in this grave for twenty-eight years. He was the father who never held his baby daughter or never even knew she was conceived. She wept because she never knew him and because his life was taken from her in a very brutal way.

Quinn sat there in despair, wanting to change the past but unable to bring back what was lost forever.

She loved the man who raised her and was all that a father could be to a daughter who wasn't naturally his.

Before him, her mother had loved this man. She had wanted to bear him a child of his own. Quade had been separated from his wife. Her mother and he had planned to marry when the divorce became final. He was brutally murdered before that could happen and Quinn was born eight months later.

No one was ever convicted of the crime. Maybe it was time to solve the mystery of her father's murder and lay to rest the unanswered questions. At the time of the murder, the local police department wasn't capable of investigating such a major crime. They handled a few robberies from time to time. A break-in occasionally, traffic infractions, spousal abuse, and bar fights but nothing even close to murder.

When Quinn arrived home she found her mother in the kitchen peeling potatoes and humming to herself.

"Where have you been all day?" asked her mom.

"I've been reacquainting myself with Grey Falls River. There have been quite a few changes since I was here. When did they make the library into a restaurant?"

"Goodness, that must have been a few years ago. It seems to do a good business. Your father and I go there for lunch or dinner every couple of weeks. A friend of ours bought it and says it is doing quite well. The bar is in the basement and they have a band on weekends."

"Where's Dad?" Quinn sat at the table and absently ate a cookie while watching her mother take a roast out of the refrigerator and begin preparing it. She was amazed how much her mom had aged in the few months since she had seen her. Remy Morrison had always been trim and attractive. Today she looked a bit haggard and tired.

"Dad is at the Elks Club doing some painting. It has needed some renovations and he is on the committee. He should be on his way home any minute. He wouldn't want to miss dinner!"

"Are you feeling okay, Mom?" Quinn asked. "You look a little tired. I'm worried you try to do too much with this big house and all your outside activities."

"Nonsense," replied her mother. "I've been taking care of this house and your dad for a long time. I'm just showing my age a little. I was working in the garden before you came and perhaps I overdid it a little. Goodness, don't worry about me, sweetie."

At that moment, Archer, walked in, grabbing his wife around the waist and swinging her around before planting a big kiss on her smiling face.

"How are my two favorite girls today? Is supper ready or do I have time for a quick shower?"

"Just make it quick," his wife answered, swatting at his retreating backside with a dishtowel.

Quinn took the plates out of the cupboard and set the table. The familiar plates with their flowered pattern brought old memories to mind of sitting at this cherished maple table so many years ago. Her parents had always insisted the family enjoy at least one meal together everyday. It was a tradition she would follow someday when she had a family.

That startled her into remembering she hadn't called Brick since she arrived. She had promised she would do that.

Before she could excuse herself and go to her apartment, her mother called to her that Brick had phoned and wanted her to call him as soon as possible.

Quinn told her mom she would be right back to help her with dinner and hurried out the door and up the stairs to her apartment.

Brick answered on the first ring. "It appears to me that a day has passed and I am finally hearing you arrived safely? Must be you have found something or someone much more important than your husband!"

"I am sorry. It just slipped my mind, oh great one! My parents were at the airport when I arrived and I just forgot all about you."

By this time Quinn was chuckling and Brick was giving her that deep rumbling roar that made him such a delight to listen to.

"I am so glad I am so easily forgettable," he said while trying to sound angry but failing to hide a chuckle in his voice.

Quinn talked for awhile, promised she would call again in a few days and then said goodbye. She loved that man so much and she knew he loved her too but for some reason they just couldn't make a marriage work.

She retired to her place after dinner dishes were done and put away. She had some research to do regarding her real father's death and wanted to know a few details before discussing the incident with her mother.

Quinn had two half sisters and one half brother who were much older than she. They were grown when their mother divorced their father and began dating Quade. She would call each of them and get their version of what happened. She would start there.

It wasn't easy to just begin investigating a twenty-eight-year-old murder case. Her mother probably still had old newspapers and other information about Quade's death. She could probably get copies from the town newspaper.

She wasn't real close to her extended family members but she loved them all. They had always supported her and attended all her activities in school. When she went away to college, Emily had written to her and sent her money every now and then.

When she married Brick, it was too far away for them to attend. It was sudden and she didn't really give anyone enough notice to go all the way to Los Angeles.

CHAPTER SIX

Emily Kidder Mack was a lovely woman who was admired for her willingness to always be available to help someone in need. She had a husband who was crazy about her and three children and four grandchildren who adored her.

She lived about twenty-five miles from her mother in a town called Putnam. She agreed wholeheartedly to meet her half sister, Quinn.

It had been a long time. She was anxious to see her and spend some time catching up.

Emily's husband, Casey, was in the lumber business. They had been childhood sweethearts. They had been married for twenty-four years. They lived on property adjacent to the sawmill.

Quinn drove into the driveway, admiring the well-trimmed bushes and trees aligning the drive before approaching the large log home with the huge porch and massive stone chimney.

Before she even parked, Emily was running out of the house, her apron flapping, arms outstretched, rushing to hug her sister.

"My word, how long has it been?" she cried, enveloping Quinn in a great bear hug.

"I don't know, sister dear, but we will never find out if you crush all the air out of my lungs and I die right here on the spot!" Quinn was laughing and crying at the same time while clearly trying to catch her breath at the same moment.

"You look fantastic, Quinn. Come inside and let's get a drink and settle in on the porch for a nice visit. Casey is out in the woods but he will be back later if you can stay for dinner. The kids will want to see you too."

"I really want to see everyone. I can't imagine how big the kiddos are now. You look absolutely happy and content. I love your house and what you have done. You are so good at making it cozy and welcoming."

"Thanks, but let's talk about you and Brick, what you've been up to miss big time Federal Prosecutor!"

"Brick and I are still living apart. We talk almost everyday and he is keeping the dog while I am here on vacation. Enough of that, I want to know what's going on with you and your family!"

Emily made them lunch and they chatted about the children's activities and looked at recent pictures of the grandchildren. The afternoon was waning when Quinn finally turned the subject around to the real reason she had come.

"Em, I really want to know about my real father's death. I know you were just a young woman and newly married at the time but perhaps you could tell me a little about the circumstances that lead up to his being murdered. Did you know his ex wife?"

"No, I didn't. I do know mom said she was very jealous and extremely possessive of Quade. She was quite a drinker and liked to gamble. Some of the people she hung out with were not well liked. She had a threatening manner and was quite aggressive. Some townspeople insist to this day that she murdered Quade."

'Do you think she did?" Quinn asked.

"No, I don't think she was the killer. After the shooting, she ran outside and collapsed. A neighbor found her and called the ambulance. Of course the police responded too. She was incoherent and finally, she passed out. You can find all this information in the old newspaper files, Quinn. Why are you interested in this after all these years?"

"I was at the cemetery today. It seems a shame that the killer was never caught and prosecuted. I know all fingers pointed to your dad, Emily. What do you think about that?"

"Cindy and I both thought of my dad when we first heard the news. In fact we went to the place where he was working and confronted him. He was visibly upset and very disturbed because he was getting all kinds of flack from co-workers about the murder. His boss gave him two weeks off until things died down a bit. He said he had no part of it and I believed him."

"Where was he the night of the murder?"

"Supposedly he was at the bar that he and mom owned at one time. Ben was there with him and provided the alibi."

The school bus came into view and that's where the conversation ended. Quinn greeted the grandchildren and soon after, Casey and the nieces arrived and dinner preparations began. Emily told Quinn they would talk again soon. Quinn left with many questions still unanswered but feeling better equipped to talk with her mother about her father's death.

The evening was warm and just the kind of night you want to sit out by the nearest lake and roast a few wieners and marshmallows. Thank goodness her parents were doing just that in their own backyard. Quinn changed into a pair of jeans and joined them.

"Where have you been all day?" asked Remy.

"I drove out to visit Emily and her family. I stayed for dinner so I could see Casey and the kiddos. I know I had dinner but I can't resist the smell of those hot dogs!" She grabbed a stick and was soon cooking her hot dog and a few marshmallows followed that.

"Oh, I love to see the fireflies. We never see them in California. Remember when I would catch them in a jar? I loved watching them as I laid in bed before I fell asleep. These are the things I miss even though I'm grown up."

"Quinn," her dad said, while rising to his feet and stretching, "you always loved the outdoors. We could hardly get you to go in the house at night. Sometimes we just put up a tent and camped outside just to get you to settle down and go to sleep."

"Don't encourage her, dear, or you'll be up in the rafters dragging that old tent out here," laughed her mother.

"It's okay, I'm ready for bed tonight. It's been a very eventful day and I'm ready to read a few chapters and put the lights out. Tomorrow is another day."

Quinn tried to read for awhile but decided to work on her laptop. Brick had sent a lengthy email about his upcoming trip to Indonesia on location for a movie. It wouldn't be until she was back in San Diego.

Penny had written to say she had compiled quite a bit of material for her regarding her father's death. She would have it for her if she attended the alumni committee meeting the following evening at the Elks Lodge.

She had a few messages from colleagues at work. They missed her but were hoping she was resting and enjoying her vacation.

Little did they know she was working on a murder case right here in Grey Falls River. Brick called her Nancy Drew when she became too personally involved in a murder case she was prosecuting.

Quinn knew her mother had some old newspaper clippings about Quade's murder. Her mother hadn't said too much about it when Quinn was curious about her dad as a teenager. The explanation was limited to the fact he was killed by someone and the killer was never apprehended. Quinn knew her parents weren't married at the time, but she carried her father's name at her mother's insistence from the day she was born.

It seemed strange to Quinn that the murderer wasn't caught. Most murders were acts of vengeance or passion. Some were planned in advance while most were spur of the minute acts of violence brought on by emotional distress.

From what she new of her father, he was one of the nicest guys in town. Everyone always had kind words to say about him. Her mother thought he was a wonderful man and said he would have loved to raise a child.

Quinn knew she would have loved him too. She had daydreamed about having him as her dad as a little girl. Her mom had said he was a better than average baseball player. When she played softball she pretended he was coaching her. She practiced hard after school and during the summer. She made the all-stars every year. It was her way of proving to her real dad that she was worthy of being his daughter.

Quinn went to sleep that night thinking of her dad and wishing she had the chance to know him better. He was taken away and she had to find out why.

CHAPTER SEVEN

P enny Stovall was president of the Grey Falls River High School Class of 2002. This year was their tenth reunion. The alumni meetings were held in a room at the Grey Falls River Elks Club once a month at seven in the evening.

The events this year included a corn roast at the home of one of the graduates, an informal get together on Friday night, and a dinner dance on Saturday evening. A lot of hours had been put into the planning by the twelve-member committee.

Penny was excited that Quinn was in town and would be attending the last meeting before the reunion. Members who lived in town were to be credited for doing all of the work. Penny knew Quinn would be the first to congratulate them on a job well done. That would raise their spirits and make them feel that their hardwork was appreciated.

The committee was expecting about 125 classmates and their dates to attend the festivities. They had compiled a list of places to stay in town and tonight they would have replies from the bed and breakfasts, hotels, and inns as to how many reservations had been made.

Penny checked her bag to see if she had everything she needed for the meeting. She had a separate packet for Quinn with information about the murder of Quade Reaghan. She had spoken to her boss about Quinn's interest. He had known Quade personally. Penny was surprised when he mentioned his concern about the safety of delving into the past of this heinous deed.

Penny had only thought it was a whim of Quinn's to do a little research. She certainly never gave a thought to it being a danger to her friend. If she knew anything at all about

Quinn, the aging publisher would be her first contact.

Quinn was the last to arrive. Everyone greeted her warmly and said they were pleased she was in town and helping with the decorations and planning.

The meeting was called to order and business was discussed and last minute checks written for supplies.

Seventy-six reservations had been recorded so far. Andy Henton said he knew two couples who would be staying with him. Stella Runyon stated another four would be at her lake house. The count would be pretty close to what the committee anticipated.

The meeting adjourned at nine. Most were headed for the bar to have a few drinks and socialize. Quinn begged off saying she had to meet with someone.

She walked with Penny to her car. Penny was telling her the publisher's reaction. Quinn looked thoughtful before replying.

"I have never considered this a dangerous game. It's been 28 years for heavens sake!

43

Who would possibly be threatened? How well do you know your boss?"

Penny put down her purse and case on the back of her car and turned toward Quinn. "I have worked at the newspaper for over five years. I have known, Glen Marti, most of my life. He and his wife are friends with my parents. Maybe it was just something he said without thinking. I don't know Q, but be careful and think about what you're doing and who you are asking questions about. Keep in mind this is a small town. Okay?"

"Gee, Penny, now you're making me even more curious about what happened. The lawyer in me is about to explode with questions. Am I hot on a trail for a killer when I don't even know the whole story? Are there people out there ready to do me in if I get close to discovering what really happened to my dad? Tell your publisher friend I will definitely be in to talk to him!"

Penny handed Quinn the information she had gathered and the two shared a hug and parted ways.

Quinn went home and began to pour over the documents. The more she read the more she wanted to know. The one article described an armored car robbery that happened eight months before Quade was killed. The police said they were investigating that as a possible connection to the crime.

"Are you kidding me?" thought Quinn. 'What on earth did one have to do with the other? This case was becoming more complicated by the minute."

The next morning Quinn emailed Brick and asked him to get information for her regarding the armored car robbery. She gave him the date and other details and he promised to get back to her within a day or two. He didn't ask her why she wanted the information and for that she was thankful. She didn't need a lecture from him about minding her business and staying away from trouble.

Her parents were playing golf this morning so after tidying up her apartment she went in search of a tennis partner at the country club. She lucked out as she discovered the local high school champion hitting some practice balls. He was a young guy, eighteen, and very good looking. He had a great smile and said he would be happy to play her a few sets.

Quinn was a good tennis player. She beat him one set but he dominated the next two. She thanked him for playing and showered and dressed and went to see if she could meet her parents for lunch.

When she walked into the dining room she immediately spotted her mother waving at her. Her dad was walking toward her at a pretty fast clip. She wondered what was going on as he grabbed her elbow and steered her back outside.

"Your mother just heard from a few friends that you are in town to investigate the death of Quade Reaghan. Is this true?" he demanded of her.

"Oh, Dad, that is the silliest thing I've heard today. What is it with this town and Quade's murder? Is everyone paranoid, or what? I've asked a few questions and all of a sudden I've become a pariah? Give me a break!" Quinn turned and walked back into the club and straight to her mother.

"Mom, I don't want you to be upset. It is my right to find out what I can about my real father's death. You can provide the answers or I can ask everyone in town. Now let's sit quietly and have a civilized lunch and pretend we are one happy family."

By this time her father had taken his seat and was gesturing the waiter to come take their order.

"Quinn is right, Remy. It's time we put an end to this speculation and give Quinn the answers she seeks. Now let's end this conversation and talk about something else."

That ended all that excitement for one afternoon. The rest of the meal was spent talking about the golf game and local gossip about the new golf pro.

CHAPTER EIGHT

Remy knew her daughter would be more than curious one day and would want to delve into the murder of her father. It had been a hurtful time for Remy. She had loved Quade. To tell the truth, she hadn't been surprised that he was murdered. His estranged wife, Corinne, had been a very hateful woman. She had threatened Remy more than once to get out of Quade's life. One evening she had even come to the restaurant where Remy worked with Remy's ex-husband, Hank. She strode right up to Remy jabbed her finger into her chest and made the remark that Remy could have Quade for one year but then she had to give him back. That was very strange at the time but it was a year and a week later that

Quade was killed. The coincidence was just too weird.

Remy's ex-husband was dating Corinne from time to time. He was the police's number one suspect in the crime. He had an alibi but if you took a poll of everyone in Grey Falls River, Hank would have been the number one person responsible.

Corinne Reaghan ended her life two months after the murder. It was rumored that she left a note admitting the crime but it was never proven.

Remy got on with her life. She had never gotten the chance to tell Quade she was pregnant. She had regretted that the entire pregnancy.

Quinn looked a lot like her father. Tall, thin, and blonde, she was his image. He would have adored her.

Archer had been a wonderful stepfather. Her children by her first marriage had accepted Quinn immediately. They doted on her and she loved them unconditionally.

Remy had been too caught up in her own grief to care who had murdered Quade. She had her suspicions but even though she had been questioned by the police, she kept them to herself.

Following the murder, she had been given police protection for a short time. The police thought if the perpetrator wanted Quade dead, maybe Remy was the next target.

Corinne had been found incoherent and semiconscious by a neighbor shortly after the murder. A neighbor had found her stumbling around her yard where she collapsed.

Remy always wondered why she wasn't killed too. She was obviously present at the time of the crime. Could she have shot her husband in the back twice with a shotgun? Quade was a big guy and fully capable of taking a gun away from a woman.

Corinne had said a realtor was coming over to look at the house. Remy and Quade were about to sit down to dinner when Quade received the call. He had left soon after to go to his home and meet the guy. That sounded like a setup but nothing was ever proven and no realtor came forward and said he was the one at the house. A lot of unanswered questions. The State Police offered their services as well as their lab for forensic testing but their offer was declined by the Grey Falls River Police Department. The Grey Falls police chief had also been dating Corinne Reaghan. Did he have anything to do with the crime? He left town and moved south a few months later. The story just became stranger and stranger.

Remy met Archer when Quinn was two. He had grown children of his own but he loved Remy and fell in love with her little girl. He knew of the love affair with Quade and often tried to get Remy to open up about the circumstances surrounding his death. Parts of the story were as mysterious today as they were at the time of the murder.

Quinn grew up and went to college and became a lawyer and then a government prosecutor. Remy was so proud of her.

Archer and Remy didn't know what to make of their daughter's relationship with Brick

Rainwater. The separation was real enough but yet they were in constant contact with each other.

Remy knew if Brick even had a clue Quinn was getting involved with this murder business he would have an absolute fit. Remy wondered if she should make a phone call but thought better of it. She didn't want to create waves. She had enough to deal with trying to keep Quinn from getting too involved.

The number one reason was she didn't trust her ex-husband. If he had been involved, he was just apt to cause trouble. He had a reputation for being a mean son of a bitch. It had been a very bitter divorce. They had married when Remy became pregnant while still in high school. Hank had been older and was out of school when they had met.

By the time they had three small children, he was out running around and Remy never knew where he was, what bar, or who he was with. She continued to stay with him until the kids were raised. That's what women did back then.

Hank was a womanizer, a gambler, and a man who loved to associate with less than acceptable men of society. It was rumored that he had friends in the Mafia and was often seen at gambling places in the larger cities. It didn't bother him to make threats or pick a fight with anyone who crossed him.

Hank had an unsavory past and the last thing Remy wanted was for Quinn and him to cross paths.

There was a time when Remy and Hank had owned a bar and grill. Remy was sure the money to purchase it had come from a payoff. She worked hard to make the place a success while Hank just stood behind the bar drinking with his cronies or playing golf with his buddies.

Remy was a good-looking woman and she had an outgoing personality. She began to date on the side just because she was starved for attention. Hank was always doing things without her. He only cared how much money they were taking in. Remy suspected he was dealing drugs on the side. She often witnessed strange transactions being done after hours at the bar. If she had questioned her husband she would probably have been back-handed and told to mind her own business.

Eventually, Hank found out about her affairs and threw her out of the house. They sold the restaurant and split the proceeds. Remy went her way and Hank went his.

Remy found happiness with Quade but it was short lived. Just how much Hank had to do with that was unknown.

She eventually married Archer and Hank remarried as well. Ironically his wife looked remarkably like Remy. They saw each other at their children's weddings and other family gatherings but seldom spoke. Occasionally, Hank would drink too much and make comments, usually demeaning, about her. He was an embarrassment so many times she soon told her kids not to invite them to the same function.

Quinn knew most of this stuff. Her sisters and brother accepted their father and wanted to include him in their lives but it remained difficult.

What would happen if Quinn continued to pursue this case and found Hank guilty of this heinous crime? How would her family react?

The last thing she wanted to do was split up her family. Would sides be taken or were they all mature enough to handle the truth?

CHAPTER NINE

Quinn awoke knowing today was her meeting with the publisher of the local newspaper. She couldn't help but wonder why he had made those remarks to Penny. Who would care that she was asking a few questions about the murder of her father? Twenty-eight years had passed! Maybe he was more concerned for something that threatened him. Her parents had both known him since high school. He was a passing friend but not close by any means.

Remy said he was quite nasty when she was at the funeral home making arrangements and he showed up to ask her some questions. What kind of person does that? He was trying to get a story out of her. Apparently it didn't matter to him that she was grieving the loss of the man she loved.

The funeral director, who was a close friend, asked him to leave. He told him it wasn't an appropriate time.

In Quinn's mind he was fishing for details that hadn't been revealed by the police.

It would be an interesting interview. Quinn was looking forward to it.

She dressed in a black suit with matching heels. One of her court outfits. It was meant to intimidate and it did just that in a number of cases. It was a sober and serious wardrobe choice. It definitely presented a look that challenged those who had sworn to tell the truth in court.

Breakfast was a quick chai tea and a piece of toast. Her appointment was at nine and she wanted to be prompt. Perhaps she would even beat him to his office. That would put him at a disadvantage right off the bat. She chuckled to herself as she belted her seatbelt and started the engine.

Glen Marti was an overweight, overbearing, and arrogant man somewhere in his early sixties. He had a receding hairline and quite a paunch. He kept her waiting in an outer office a few minutes. She had seen him walking swiftly from the parking lot while glancing at his watch. Apparently he had a back door into his office as he didn't pass her as she was waiting.

They had exchanged pleasantries. He was asking about her parents and how happy she must be to be visiting.

Following her response, Quinn, got right to the point of her visit.

"Mr. Marti, I am here to ask you why you remarked to my friend, Penny, that you think my looking into my father's murder might be a dangerous undertaking."

"Please, call me Glen. I didn't mean it as a threat, Ms. Reaghan. I merely made the comment as a reminder that this case was never solved and there could be people out there who were involved and may not want anyone delving into their past."

"I would say, if that were the case, they must have something to hide," Quinn replied. "What do you know about the crime?"

Glen spun his chair and looked out the window for a moment before responding. "I knew both Quade and his wife, Corinne. I knew the marriage was not a happy one. Corinne was older than Quade. She had a tendency to run his life. He was his own person, very quiet until he drank and then he became talkative and easily brought to a state of anger."

Quinn stood and walked around the room, pausing to look at the many shelves of books lining the walls of the office.

"Tell me, Glen, when my father was murdered, were you surprised?"

"You could have knocked me over with a feather. I knew Corinne was unhappy that Quade was living with your mother. Everyone in town knew that. She was a very jealous woman and often made threatening remarks about your mother. I assumed she was all talk. She was a very verbal woman. There wasn't anything quiet about her. That said, I was still astounded to hear Quade was killed in their home."

"Were you aware, Glen, that the chief of police was having an affair with Mrs. Reaghan?" Before Mr. Marti could answer, Quinn leaned over his shoulder and said quietly into his ear "were there other men, Glen? You perhaps?"

"Ms. Reaghan, that is preposterous! I have been happily married to Mary for thirty-four years! How dare you come into my office and make such a statement! If John Farraday was having an affair with Corinne Reaghan, it was his business and no one else's."

The publisher was visibly upset. Quinn returned to her seat and sat quietly for a moment allowing the man across from her to regain his composure.

"I apologize, sir, for upsetting you. I am searching for answers regarding the death of my dad. Sometimes I find it necessary to shock the people I am interviewing." Quinn quietly picked up her paperwork and put it in her briefcase.

Glen arose from his chair behind his desk and walked around in front and sat on the corner of the desk. "You had me going there, counselor, for the moment. No, I never dated Corinne. She was a bit too aggressive for my taste. She was not a refined woman by any stretch of the imagination. Some men may prefer their women rough, but I'm not one of them. Thanks for coming in and talking to me. My door is always open if you have any questions or need any information I might have at my disposal."

He held out his hand and Quinn shook it, giving him a big smile and a final remark.

"I appreciate your candor, Mr. Marti. I did not mean to offend you. I am sure I will upset a lot of apple carts in my quest to find the killer of my father. I am not afraid to ask questions. If that is a threat to some people, then they must be the ones who are afraid. Thank you very much for your time. I can see myself out."

Quinn exited the building with as much aplomb as she could muster. Se felt she was the victor in this interview. Glen Marti came into the room full of bravado but was reduced to a red-faced blubbering idiot. Funny how men came apart when asked a simple question.

Quinn's next stop was home to change into something more comfortable. She had promised her grandmother she would join her for lunch. She was taking her out to eat to a teahouse as a special treat. She was prepared to be lectured about her marriage arrangement. Her grandmother thought the whole idea of living apart was simply ridiculous and so unnecessary. She blamed everything from sleeping in a king-sized bed to women working too much, to not having children, as the reason for the breakup of marriages these days.

Perhaps she has a point, Quinn thought. It was a different world these days. She and Brick did have a king-sized bed, she did work too much, and no they didn't have kids.

Annie Wickcliff was a delight. Seventy-eight years old and as feisty as an ornery mule. Quinn loved her dearly.

When she pulled into her grandmother's driveway, the elderly lady came out the front door shaking her cane at Quinn.

"Just a minute, sweetheart," she yelled. "I'm on the phone but I'll be right there."

In a few minutes she came bustling down the steps and got into the car. Quinn was outside holding the door for her.

"My goodness, Gram, who was so important you had to have me wait," she said teasingly. "Don't tell me it was a new man in your life!"

"Silly child, it was my stockbroker. He wants to meet with me next week. A new man, who do you take me for? I do have a special man already. His name is James and we go out to dinner and to concerts and plays."

"That's wonderful, Gram. I hope I can meet him while I'm here."

"So tell me about your husband, young lady. Are you back together or are you still acting like a couple of hippies?" Her grandmother fairly spit the last words out of her mouth.

"Don't worry your pretty little head about Brick and I, Gram. We're just fine."

CHAPTER TEN

Brick Axlerod Rainwater was at that moment attempting to roust a suspect from an abandoned building near the docks in San Pedro. He was the lead detective in a case involving a death of a child. The suspect he was close to apprehending was responsible for the child's death.

Brick was tired of capturing women's boyfriends who murdered their children. It was practically an epidemic in Los Angeles.

The innocent children were the victims of these violent crimes. He hated these men with a passion. They had no defense. They didn't deserve a defense. He was a lawyer but he became a cop because he wanted these useless dregs of mankind to be caught and prosecuted. He didn't have to defend them, he could arrest them and see justice done behind bars once they were convicted. They would get what they deserved in the prison system.

The suspect came out of the building and lay spread eagled on the ground, whimpering that no one hurt him.

Just like the scum of the earth he is, thought Brick. Cowering like a whipped puppy, crying like a baby. It was all Brick could do to avoid telling him to get on his feet and fight like a man. He'd love to beat the hell out of the guy, like the guy did to a small child. Just give him the chance!

Once the guy was handcuffed and put into a patrol car, Brick got into his car and headed for the station to file his report.

On the way he was thinking how he regretted not having a child with Quinn when they were still together. They had both been too intent on having a career.

He never intended to get caught up in this movie thing. It just happened. Okay, he thought, he had enjoyed the attention. What man wouldn't have? Women fawning over him all the time. No wonder Quinn became sick of it and him. He had let himself become wrapped up in the sensationalism. He was a star! Yea, right. He was a jerk. He was full of himself and expected Quinn to worship him like the studios and the starlets.

Brick was this macho cop with an attitude. This image was magnified ten-fold by all the attention he received, onstage and in the media.

He missed his wife. This arrangement was killing him. He would do anything to get her back and be a family again. Maybe he could convince her to start a family. She would be a great mother. She had wonderful parents. Her real dad had been murdered. She didn't talk about it much but he knew it was always on her mind. Now here she was, back in the town where it all happened. This story she wanted him to check out, could she be up to something? That would be worrisome. Brick thought he had better call her today and find out what she was up to. Heaven forbid she was becoming Nancy Drew again. She loved mysteries and especially, trying to solve them.

One of these days she was going to get into trouble trying to solve a case by herself. She wasn't trained to be a detective. She was always getting involved in his cases. She pestered him to death to let her help. He finally stopped discussing his cases at home.

He knew she was up to something. He was due to leave for location in a few days. He'd better find out what was going on in Grey Falls River before he left the country.

CHAPTER ELEVEN

Quinn was out on the river fishing with her dad. She loved to fish and so did he. They had been out on the water a good two hours. She had caught several bass and a few blue gills and thrown them back. They probably had enough to have a good fish fry later on that evening.

Archer brought up the subject of her mother and Quade. He must have been pondering it for quite sometime. Quinn wasn't surprised, he had been quiet for a very long time. For him that was something as he loved to chat.

"Your mother is worried about this investigation of yours, Quinn," he remarked. "Frankly, so am I. It's been twenty-eight years and everyone has put it to rest. It doesn't matter who did it or how it happened.

The man is dead and you can't bring him back."

"I know, Dad. I'm not trying to bring him back. I want justice done. Someone in this town knows what happened that night. Everywhere I go and everyone I talk to says the same thing. Mom's ex-husband pulled the trigger. Do you think that too, dad?" Quinn put her fishing pole down and turned toward her dad who was taking a break and drinking a beer. The day was sunny and bright and the sun was hot on the water. Although her dad wore his favorite fishing hat, his face was getting a bit red. Soon they would have to call it a day and head for shore.

"Let's put it this way, sweetie, at the time I would have bet my life on it. Hank was a very tough guy. Really, everyone was afraid to cross any of the Kidder brothers. They even fought among themselves. They fought constantly over everything. If someone interfered they'd beat the crap out of them. Their mother was the only person who could control them. Old Ma Kidder ruled her family with an iron fist.

She towered over Mr. Kidder, who was a really sweet guy. How he ended up with her has always been a mystery."

One time the old lady wanted a room addition so the dining area could be larger. No one made an effort to do anything about it so one day the boys came in from work and school and found the rear end of the house torn down. Yep, she was a terror, that woman.

Hank hurt your mother from day one of the marriage. When they divorced, he was jealous of any man she dated. He hated that they split the proceeds from the restaurant and bar they owned. The divorce was bitter. He talked about her all over town. I think he began dating Corinne just for spite. They were definitely two of a kind.

"From what I heard, Ma Kidder went to her grave believing her son killed Quade Reaghan."

"I heard he was questioned by the police several times but had an alibi that was proved out to be true."

"Alibis can be bought, darling girl. His son, your half-brother, Ben, said Hank was at the bar with him and your sister, Cindy. Was he forced into saying that or is it true? Who knows? No one but those three people. Would you cover for your mom?"

Archer put his can away in the trash bag and picked up his fishing pole and began to put the bait on the hook.

"You asked if Hank was capable of murdering Quade. In my opinion yes, he was. He was an evil man. Today he's older, in ill health, but still a mean son of a gun. Stay away from him, Quinn. He's bad news. He'll pay the price some day, if he's guilty of the crime."

"What about Corinne? Do you think she committed suicide or do you think the same killer did her too?"

"That's another good question. She was going to an attorney that Monday. She was found in the garage laying down on a blanket with the motor running. The paper said she had a bump on her head. There was a note but the contents were never revealed.

71

Personally, I don't think she could have killed Quade. He was killed with a shotgun. I don't think she could have pulled the trigger twice. Quade was a big guy. He could certainly have overpowered her. Plus the repercussion after one shot would have knocked her for a loop. She wasn't a hunter. She would have had powder marks on her hands and arm. No, I definitely think it was someone else.

The media could have had a hand in her death. It was in all the papers that she was going to see an attorney. Murderers read the papers too. It could have been made to look like a suicide. Everything about this case is just too complicated. The local police department was simply out of its league trying to solve it. The police chief was not liked or respected by the officers under him. He was dating Corinne, he left town soon after the murder. He certainly didn't help the investigation. There was a report that the department's shotgun was missing and was never found. Coincidence? Once again, who knows?"

CHAPTER TWELVE

Remy announced the next morning at breakfast that she wanted to drive to New York City and visit her daughter, Cindy.

Quinn welcomed this news as it would give her the opportunity to speak to Cindy about the murder.

Archer said he didn't want to make the trip so Quinn and Remy began to make plans to go without him.

They would take Remy's car and spend a couple days making the drive. They called Cindy and she said she couldn't wait to see them. She lived alone in the city and had plenty of room for guests. If they could put up with her two cats they were most welcome to visit.

It was decided they would leave the next morning. Quinn spent the better part of the day packing a few clothes and her laptop. This would be the perfect time to get more information. Her mother would be a captive audience in the car.

She called Brick so he would know where she was going and how long she would be away from Grey Falls River. He said he wanted to discuss a few things with her but she begged off saying she had things to do. She could tell he wasn't too happy with that answer but she promised to call him from Cindy's.

The next morning they loaded the car.

Remy kissed her husband goodbye and made him promise not to eat a bunch of junk food. He loved gorging himself at the fast food restaurants whenever he was alone for a few days. He did this even though the freezer was full of homemade food his wife had prepared for just such an occasion.

Quinn agreed to let Remy drive the first few hours. It was a beautiful day to be driving across New York State. Quinn was mesmerized by the different colors of green reflected in the trees, the grasses, and the many bushes and plants along side the road.

A true artist could capture the different shades with just a stroke of the brush. Quinn was not an artist but she could appreciate the talent she found in pictures and paintings.

Remy was humming to herself and thinking about her youngest daughter. She worried about her interest in the death of her father. Perhaps this little trip would be a chance to put it to rest, a diversion for a few days at least.

Her hopes were dashed when out of the blue, Quinn threw a question at her. "So, tell me Mom, why do you think Quade was murdered?"

"For heavens sake, Quinn, I'm driving! You just sit there and think about something other than that damn murder! I almost ran the car off the road, for Pete's sake!"

"Sorry, Mom, I was just trying to get some information out of you. You've been evading the issue since I first brought it up. What's the big deal? It's been twenty-eight years and you would think you would at least be able to tell me the true story. I have been all over town asking questions from other people and my own mother refuses to tell me the real story! It's frustrating!"

Quinn disgustedly turned toward the window and slunk down in her seat.

Minutes passed before Remy finally laid her hand on Quinn's. "I'm sorry, sweetie. I really feel the past is the past and nothing can bring your father back. I know it is difficult for you not to have the answers you seek. Your dad was murdered before he even knew I was pregnant with his child. That has been foremost in my mind all these years. How I wish he had never gone over to his house that night. If I could just have those moments back."

Quinn looked at her mother's face and saw the anguish in her eyes as a tear ran slowly down her cheek. That was a defining moment for Quinn. She knew the pain her mother had been experiencing for the past twenty-eight years. She had put the past in the back of her mind. She had delivered a baby girl on her own. She endured the criticism of others and raised Quinn with pride and love and respect for her relationship with Quade Reaghan.

Maybe she should just put an end to her search. It was just such a personal need to find the killer. Her whole being would not rest until she knew who had pulled the trigger. She had to know. That was the bottom line. She had to do this.

"Mom, I am so sorry if I upset you. I know it is difficult for you that I am doing this. I promise I will not involve you in my quest for information. But, if you can help, if you can remember any detail, please tell me. I cannot stop my investigation. It is something I have to do. You just have to accept that."

Remy looked at her daughter and touched her arm as she continued to drive. "I wish you wouldn't continue this search for the truth, Quinn. I will try to help you as you seem to have your mind set on solving the case. You tell me what you know and I will try to fill in the blanks if I can remember."

The next few hours were spent with Quinn bringing her mother up to date on her findings. Most of her information came from newspaper articles and what she had learned from a few individuals. She was sure Remy could fill in many missing blanks.

Quinn relieved her mother of driving duties when they stopped for a quick lunch along the freeway. When they returned to the car, Remy remarked she would have to close her eyes and take a wee nap.

The afternoon went by quickly and when Remy awoke they were just coming into New York City.

CHAPTER THIRTEEN

Cindy was an investment banker. She had been married for several years but had been divorced for three years. She kept their apartment in New York City and her ex had the house in the suburbs. Cindy loved the hectic pace of living in the midst of the masses who lived and worked in the city.

Her apartment was quite large. It had three bedroom and three bathrooms. The living room was spacious with a wonderful view of downtown through the sliding glass door to the patio. The kitchen was off the dining room. It was designed for entertaining. Cindy had the architect put in commercial appliances. She and her husband had thrown numerous parties and loved to entertain.

The apartment had a locked entranceway and guests had to be buzzed in unless they knew the code.

When Remy and Quinn arrived, Cindy was home and expecting their arrival. She had been at the elevator to meet them after they had parked the car in the apartment's underground parking garage. Quinn carried their bags while her mother walked on ahead to greet Cindy.

The pair was welcomed with hugs and kisses. Cindy was a person just full of energy and exuberance. People wondered why she was divorced. She was all bubbly and cheerful. She made you happy just being around her. But who knows what goes on behind closed doors.

"You made good time," said Cindy as she led them down the hall to their rooms. "I didn't know whether to make dinner or wait and see what time you arrived. Would you like to go out for a bite or are you too tired? There is a terrific Italian restaurant just around the corner. We could easily walk there."

"We'd love that," Remy replied. "Just give us a few minutes to freshen up and we'll be ready. I love your apartment, dear. It's so bright and airy. Are you sure you feel comfortable living in downtown New York?"

"Now Mom, you know how I feel about the city. It's in my soul. I love it. It gives me a sense of urgency and excitement. I feel like I can do anything here. I feed off the city's energy!"

Quinn laughed and gave her sister a big hug. "I'm happy if you're happy. I prefer the quiet beach living but I understand your heart racing to the pulse the city life. It fits you."

Following their delicious dinner, the threesome enjoyed a glass of wine and listened to the piano music being played in the restaurant's lounge.

Remy began to relax from the long day's drive from Grey Falls River. Quinn was enjoying the music and at the same time thinking about how to approach Cindy on the subject of Quade's murder. She knew Cindy would defend her father to the nth degree. They had always been very close. But maybe she would welcome the chance to tell her story just to be sure Quinn understood he had not been a part of the crime.

It was after midnight when the weary travelers finally went to bed. Cindy had to work the next day but promised to be home early. Remy told her not to worry about them. They would have dinner prepared when she got home. Cindy was overjoyed to hear that. She hadn't been home to enjoy her mother's cooking for over a year.

Remy and Quinn decided to take a tour of the city. It was a guided tour that took in all the popular sights and attractions. Quinn had been in the New York City often during her years in Washington, D.C. She had been there on business and never took the time to see the sights. She and Brick had been to a few Broadway shows and of course had dined at a lot of good restaurants.

Brick had spent a lot of time in New York while making special appearances for a movie opening or a publicity event. Quinn hated those and avoided them when at all possible. The crowds and mayhem unnerved her. Brick loved it. He was a people person while she was more of an introvert and respected her privacy.

Remy wanted to stop at a local market and pick up a few of Cindy's favorite foods. The market was a bustling place. You could hear a dozen different languages being spoken while standing in the checkout line. Quinn was used to the blend of voices but her mother was intrigued by the musical rhythm of the different dialects.

"It's like being in a concert hall and hearing a dozen different songs being played at the same time," she mused. "It's thrilling but confusing."

Quinn chuckled and squeezed her mother's hand. "You're a real keeper, you know that?"

Cindy was home when they returned. Dinner was delicious. Remy watched the news while Quinn and Cindy cleaned up the kitchen. Remy admitted she was exhausted from the day's events and wanted to take a hot bath and go to bed.

Cindy and Quinn decided to head out to a few clubs. Cindy was quite a few years older than Quinn but she knew the New York scene and where to go for fun. Nothing wild or crazy, just a couple piano bars where they could enjoy a few drinks and listen to some wonderful music.

Before Quinn could decide how to bring up the subject of the murder, Cindy took a drink and as she set her glass down on the table she gave a long sigh and began to speak. "I know why you came with mom. It wasn't just to see me, but I'm glad you did. I know you are investigating the murder of your dad. I can try to answer any questions you have. I don't think I can offer much, but I'm willing to help if I can."

"Thanks, Cindy. Truthfully, I didn't know how to approach the subject. It's been a very long time since the crime was committed. You were in college at the time. I know how close you are to your dad. I don't want you to feel that I'm out to accuse him of anything. I'm simply looking for answers. It's a murder that was committed out of passion and should have been easily solved, but for some strange reason, the police work was a disgrace. I have several suspects, a dead wife, no weapon, no lab reports and several leads that go nowhere."

Cindy nodded her head in agreement. "It was a very strange situation. Mom was being guarded for fear that whomever killed Quade might come after her next." Cindy paused and was quiet for a few minutes. "I was at the family bar in Cherrydale with dad and my brother, Ben. I was pretty drunk and honestly couldn't tell you if my dad was there the entire night or not. I was dating the bartender at the time and my attention was divided. My parents had owned the bar for a long time and I knew everyone that came in. I could have missed something."

"When did you first hear of Quade's death?" Quinn was grateful her sister had brought up the subject but nonetheless she felt a certain evasiveness in her story.

"Emily called me after she had seen it on the evening's news. I drove to her house and we began looking for dad. I know you're thinking why did we immediately suspect dad? I guess it was just a gut reaction. His ex-wife was living with the guy and he had an intense dislike of my mother at that time."

"Had your dad ever threatened your mother or Quade when you were in his presence?" Quinn spoke right to the point.

"My dad was a drunk. I won't kid you about that. He was a mean drunk. He often shot off his mouth about mom and Quade. He hated them both and yes, he made threats but he did that a lot about certain people who had offended him in one way or the other. Let's face facts. My dad was a gambler. He had contacts in Buffalo who were mixed up in illegal gambling and who knows what else. He was not a well respected man in the community. Of course we suspected him!"

Quinn waited a few minutes before speaking. She was impressed by Cindy's candidness concerning her dad. She was right though. Her father had never been an upstanding man about town. She had often heard stories growing up how her mom had worked her butt off at the bar and restaurant while her husband sat at the bar drinking and socializing with his cronies or off golfing and gambling.

"Did you speak to your mother first or your dad?"

"We tried to call mom but she had a friend with her and she told us mom was too distraught to answer any questions. We said we would be by later. My aunt had arrived and the police were coming and going so we went looking for dad. We found him at work but he was very upset because everyone at work was accusing him of the murder. We hardly got to speak to him before the police arrived and took him to the station for questioning. He swore to Emily and I that he hadn't done it. We took him at his word and left him alone. What else could we do?"

"What's your opinion today, twenty-eight years later? Quinn asked.

"I don't know who shot Quade. I honestly don't. My dad could have done it but it doesn't make sense that he would be at a bar drinking with us, leave and drive to Grey Falls River, shoot a man twice in the back with a shotgun, drive back to the bar and act as if nothing had happened. What kind of person could do such a thing and show no effects from it? Dad isn't a hardened criminal or a trained assassin!"

Quinn thanked Cindy for being so forthright. She didn't want to press her sister any further so she changed the subject. Soon they went home and retired for the night. Quinn had a difficult time getting to sleep as the entire conversation kept running through her mind. She knew her sister was having the same problem.

CHAPTER FOURTEEN

The next day was Saturday so the three women decided to spend the day shopping. Cindy insisted on buying her mother a new outfit and then treating them to lunch. They had a delightful day together. That evening Cindy surprised them with tickets to a Broadway show. She had rented a limousine and the three of them enjoyed a wonderful evening.

Brick called Quinn just as they were exiting the limo at the theater. He was anxious to speak to Quinn but he spent the next few minutes talking to Cindy. He told her he missed the fun times they had shared with her and her ex-husband, Joe. By the time their conversation ended, they had to hurry to take their seats.

Sunday, all the ladies slept in until after ten. Cindy suggested they dress comfortably and go for a ride in the country and stop for brunch at a quaint restaurant one of her friends owned. The restaurant was in a complex that included an antique store, a homemade candy shop, plus a clothing boutique.

Remy loved antiques so while she was happily browsing the store, Cindy and Quinn checked out the clothing boutique. Quinn found the perfect dress for the alumni reunion and dance. It was light blue to match her eyes. The material was chiffon and so light she felt like she was wearing feathers. She felt like a fairy princess when she tried it on. It fit perfectly. The boutique had jewelry that matched the dress and she found sandals too. She was delighted with her purchases.

When everyone met up to go to brunch, they found they had all bought something they liked. Remy's was the biggest purchase. They didn't know how they would fit it in the car. It was an antique breadbox, beautifully handcrafted.

It had a window with hand-painted apples on it. It fit into the trunk for now but with the luggage it would have to be moved into the back seat.

The brunch was wonderful. Cindy's friend, Sally, was a delightful lady. She gave them a seat overlooking the little lake. The food was delicious. Homemade breads and desserts and fresh fruits and vegetables from nearby gardens and orchards.

The weekend had been spectacular but the next day they were headed back to Grey Falls River. Their time with Cindy had been so much fun. They promised to come back again.

The drive home was uneventful. When they pulled into the driveway they were both ready for a few days of inactivity to get their lives back to normal. Quinn had several messages reminding her of the reunion committee's next meeting. Remy was just happy to be back home with her husband to stop the fast food binge he had been on during her absence.

CHAPTER FIFTEEN

Quinn had returned Brick's phone calls when she returned home Sunday from their day in the country. He had cautioned her on continuing to pursue this case. He was worried she'd get herself into a real mess if she continued to question people she didn't even know.

She assured him she wasn't taking any unnecessary risks, after all this case was twenty-eight years old! Brick knew better. Give Quinn an inch and she would track you down and force you into telling her things you didn't even think you knew. Quinn was a pit bull when she wanted information.

Grey Falls River was preparing for its bicentennial. The high school reunion for every graduating class was being held the same weekend. The returning alumni could enjoy the bicentennial festivities as well as the school reunion. The classes celebrating special year reunions planned special parties to celebrate their year.

There were concerts in the park, art displays all over town, a play at the local theater, a carnival, vintage car rally, and many other events.

Remy and Archer were volunteers on a float building project for the local Elks Lodge. Remy had made them costumes depicting the colonial era they would be wearing on the float. It promised to be a very entertaining weekend, Quinn thought as she passed the back of the Elks and spotted her parents and other members climbing all over an old hay wagon.

Quinn was on her way to visit an old friend from high school. Took Ryder had joined the marines just out of high school. When he was discharged he went to school and studied criminal justice and then joined the Grey Falls River police department. He had happily agreed to meet with Quinn and discuss the old case she was investigating.

Took Ryder was still a very handsome man. He came striding up to her in his uniform looking like a model for Police Monthly. Quinn was used to seeing a man in a police uniform. She was still married to one for goodness sake. It still made her heart fill with pride to see a man in uniform.

"Hi stranger!" Took said as he enveloped her in a hug that took her breath away. "You are just as beautiful as ever. How's that movie star husband of yours? I didn't think you'd ever want to leave Hollywoood," he said drawing out the name.

"Brick is just fine. You aren't doing so bad yourself, Took. How's your family?"

Took removed his cap and ran his fingers through his red wavy hair and grinned from ear to ear. "Just great. We have two boys and Janis is expecting again. It's a girl this time and we are thrilled to death."

"Took, that's wonderful. Please tell Janis hello for me and give her and the boys a hug. I will see her at the class reunion soon and deliver one personally."

Quinn followed Took into the police station and he motioned for her to take a seat in his office. He then closed the door and took a seat behind his desk.

"I knew you were coming so I took the time to do some preliminary checking on that old case. Frankly, Quinn, it leaves a lot of blank spaces that were never filled in. For one thing, why didn't the then chief of police accept the help offered by the state police and local FBI? This murder was way over the local police department's capabilities. It looks suspicious to me but I don't know much about the case or how everything went down. Perhaps you can fill me in on what you know."

"It was a very strange case, Took. My mother told me the story quite a few years ago but I never had the time to check into it until I took a break from my job and came home for awhile this summer. I've always wanted to delve into the case because it has so many unanswered questions. You probably know as much as I do but let me fill you in as best I can."

CHAPTER SIXTEEN

Quinn spent the next three hours going over the case with Sergeant Ryder. He was amazed at the hours she had spent interviewing so many of the townspeople and family. He cautioned her on interfering where she might not be welcome. He would see what he could do to help but she wasn't to take the law into her own hands. She promised her friend she would simply continue her investigating behind the scenes.

Took told her the case was closed. A suicide note was found with the deceased wife and a confession of the murder of Quade was included in that note. At the time there was no reason to conclude anything different so that was that.

No, the gun had never been found. No, the circumstances of the wife's suicide were never questioned. It was a closed case. End of story.

It wasn't the end of the story as far as Quinn was concerned. She didn't believe for one minute that Corinne Reaghan killed herself or that she had killed her husband.

There was a lot more to this story. Why didn't the police chief want help? Why did he leave town a few months later? He was a local guy but he never came back for the school reunion. He used to be on the alumni committee, her mother said. Now he never comes. There must be a reason, Quinn thought.

Quinn hadn't spoken to her half-brother, Ben. He wasn't as close to her as her half-sisters. Ben kept to himself. He was married and had a son. He had married late in life. Quinn liked his wife. She had tamed Ben down through the years. He had been wild and crazy like his father, Hank Kidder. It wouldn't be easy asking him questions. He was not a real sociable guy.

Plus he was very defensive of his dad. Quinn doubted that he would have much to offer but she felt she should cover her bases and ask him anyway.

Ben's wife, Carrie, answered the phone when Quinn called. Ben was playing golf but she told Quinn she could meet him at the country club and he'd probably be in the bar if he was done playing.

Quinn didn't have anything planned for the afternoon so she headed up to the golf course. It was a gorgeous day. It was warm with just enough breeze to be comfortable. Grey Falls River was a small town but it boasted a lovely eighteen-hole golf course.

The course was completed in the early sixties. The front nine holes were farmland but the back nine holes were carved out of the woods. Golfers came from all around the area. It was a par 71 for eighteen holes. They loved the course because it was scenic and was moderately difficult to play. You had to be accurate on the fairways as they were narrow because of the woods.

Quinn was interested in seeing the golf course because Quade's house had backed right up to it. The course was searched thoroughly for the shotgun used in his murder. Quinn often thought how far could Corinne have thrown it before she was discovered by the neighbor. It would certainly have been found. The back of their property wasn't even in the wooded section. Just another unanswered question.

Quinn got to the clubhouse just as Ben was on the first tee. He gestured her over and told her to jump in his golf cart and ride the course with him.

"What brings you out on this beautiful day, sister poo?" Ben asked as he jumped into the cart after teeing off. He put his arm around her and gave her shoulders a squeeze. "I haven't had the chance to ask you out to the house to see Carrie and Chance. Sorry about that."

Quinn was a bit surprised by his pleasantness but she hadn't seen him in a long time. Married life has been good for him, she thought.

"I wanted to see you, silly boy. I have some questions for you. Play your game and we'll talk when you're done playing."

"Let's talk as I play. Chance has a scout meeting tonight and I am helping with their project so it's now or never sweetheart!"

Quinn thought it was best to just jump right in and begin the questions she had prepared. "Ben, what do you know about my father's death? I mean, I'm trying to learn how it happened and who was involved. I know your dad was a suspect but the police concluded that it was done by his wife, Corinne, and then she killed herself. Do you believe that's how it went down?"

Ben didn't answer right away. He drove the cart off the fairway, into a grove of trees and turned the ignition off.

"I would like to say that's what happened but you and I both know better. I don't know what happened. I wasn't there. I do know my father didn't do it. He may have been a part of it but he wasn't the trigger man. He wasn't angry with Quade. He hated my mother but he had no reason to kill Quade Reaghan. Quade's wife was a vindictive, angry bitch. She couldn't stand the thought of Quade living with my mother. I am convinced she wanted Quade dead, my mother too, but I am positive she didn't shoot him."

"Ben, you are so sure of what you're saying. I have to believe you are telling me the truth. Who do you think pulled the trigger?"

"Quinn, some people in town swear it was a friend of Corinne. Others will say it was her son. Many think it was my dad. My own grandmother went to her grave thinking her son was the hitman. We could never convince her otherwise. Corinne wasn't lily white. She ran with a bad bunch. She loved to gamble, horse racing was a bad habit of hers. She hung out at a lot of bad places with a lot of disreputable people. I know because my dad told me. He saw her a few times. She wasn't a nice person. It was a shame your father was killed and never got to know you. I am real sorry about that. The killing about destroyed my mother. I know she's happy she has you. I liked Quade. He didn't deserve to die. I know you want to find the answers. Talk to my dad. I know you don't know him and you've heard all kinds of stories about him, bad ones mostly. If you want, I'll make the arrangements."

"Thanks, Ben. I would love to talk to him and see what he has to say. He's a vital part of my investigation. Thanks for talking to me. I hope we can get together before I leave. I'd love to have everyone together."

"It's a done deal, sis. Let's finish this round and I'll buy you a drink at the clubhouse."

CHAPTER SEVENTEEN

Brick was concerned that Quinn was going to pursue the cold case murder of her father until she got what she wanted. He had heard from various family members and friends about Quinn's intense interest in finding out every last detail of the crime. He was worried someone would harm her if she stepped on one too many toes. He knew from experience that the one responsible for the crime would go to any lengths to end the investigation.

Quinn was all but ignoring his phone calls and text messages. If he wanted to stop this mission of hers, he would have to make a trip to Grey Falls River.

His last movie had wrapped up last week. He had made the decision that it was his last picture. He was ready to settle down and raise a family. Everyday it was a new worry with Quinn and this search she was undertaking. It made him realize how important she was to him.

He had been selfish getting caught up in his own self worth. The travel, the glitz, and the glamor didn't mean a thing at the end of the day when he came home to an empty house.

Leading ladies were mostly interested in how they looked on the screen. They led empty lives on the set. Sure, some were happily married and had kids but it wasn't an easy life. Nannies and babysitters did not replace the mother. Too many times he dealt with crying actresses away from home who had just spoken with a crying child on the phone. A child who just wanted their mom. Money did not compensate for the presence of a parent.

Today he was having lunch with his mother. She had flown to Los Angeles from San Francisco just to pay him a visit. He knew the subject of Quinn would come up. His mother was crazy about her daughter-in-law. She blamed the separation on her son. She loved him but always told him he was self centered like his father. Brick always listened and agreed with her and she went away thinking she had done her job.

Brick chose a light blue polo shirt and light gray slacks with a pair of gray loafers. The sun was shining brightly as he exited the house. He looked down the beach and saw a family with a dog playing in the water. He thought how wonderful that would be. He was more than ready to play that role for life.

Jane Emerald Brixton was an attractive woman for being fifty-seven. Heads still turned when she walked into a room. Her hair was a vibrant gold and her eyes were as green as her favorite gemstone, the peridot. She was very slim and had a personal trainer who made sure she was a walking advertisement of his efforts.

Jane was seated at the table having a cocktail when Brick walked into the room. The maitre de recognized him immediately and led him to his seat. After seating him, the gentleman placed a menu by his plate, gave a quick bow and retreated.

"My goodness," Jane said, placing her hand over her heart, "you have even gotten more handsome since I saw you last. I am sure every woman in the restaurant has fallen in love with you!"

"Come on, Mom, get real. It hasn't been that long and I'm the same old me. I must say you are very pleasing to the eye of many a gentleman in the restaurant. You look wonderful. I'm sure Dad tells you this at least once a day."

"Jack hardly pays attention to me these days," his mother replied, looking down at her plate.

"I can't believe that. Has something happened I should know about," Brick asked, reaching for his mother's hand. A look of worry crossed his face.

"Darling, it's nothing. Just a silly old woman's fear of getting old. I think of your dad around all those young pretty girls every day and it puts my mind to wandering."

"Mother, you have nothing to worry about. Dad tells me all the time that you're the best thing that ever happened to him. He'd be lost without you. You're the love of his life."

"Thank you sweetheart." Jane's eyes were moist as she patted Brick's hand and looked him in the eye. "I wish you and Quinn could share this kind of love, like your dad and I."

"Aha," replied Brick, with a smile on his face. I knew you would get around to the subject of my marriage eventually."

"I just want my son to be happy. You and Quinn are so dear to us. We had hoped for grandchildren long before this. It's just heartbreaking, that's what it is, heartbreaking."

His mother made a big show of taking a hanky from her purse and wiping her eyes.

Brick picked up his menu and began reading the specials of the day.

"You just don't care that your father and I are getting older and lonely without having any children from you to love and shower with attention. Brick, you are shameless and uncaring. I did not raise you to be so unkind."

Brick laid the menu down on the table and took both her hands in his. "Mom, I love Quinn. I have decided to quit the movie business and try to make my marriage work. "Well, it's about time you came to your senses, son. I was beginning to think I would die before ever going to my grandchild's baptism."

"Mom, you are so dramatic. You should be the one in show business!

CHAPTER EIGHTEEN

Plans for the tenth high school reunion of Grey Falls River High School were in the final stages. Penny and the committee were going over the final lists of who would be decorating and who would be taking care of the caterers for Friday night's informal party.

Quinn listened to everyone's opinion before suggesting they have a group picture taken on Saturday night at the dance. This way everyone would be dressed up and looking their best. Plus everyone would attend on Saturday night. Some wouldn't even arrive in town until late Friday or Saturday.

Her suggestion was well received and someone volunteered to find a photographer for that event. Penny said someone from the newspaper would be available to take pictures of the weekend events for publicity.

The parade float was being built on Marilyn Birch's farm so that was discussed. The parade would be held the morning of the dinner dance. Those on the committee who wouldn't be riding on the float would be decorating.

Quinn was glad when the meeting was adjourned. She was still tired from getting up early to go fishing with Archer again. He always insisted on being on the water at first light. She tried to tell him the fish weren't even up yet at that hour but he didn't buy it.

Quinn begged off going for a drink. Her jeep looked very inviting sitting in the parking lot ready to take her home. The town was quiet, no traffic at all as she began to pull out onto the main street.

Quinn had just begun her turn onto the street when a truck came barreling around the corner and hit the left front end of the jeep, spinning the car around where it hit a pole and bounced backwards before coming to rest in the middle of the street. The truck didn't stop but raced down through town at breakneck speed.

The street didn't take long to fill with people who heard the crash and came pouring out of their homes and the club and a nearby bar.

Quinn had been knocked unconscious from the force of the airbag when it inflated. The ambulance arrived within minutes and transported her to the hospital. Penny rode with her to the hospital, telephoning her parents while en route.

While Quinn was being checked out and admitted, Remy and Archer arrived, looking very distraught and demanding to know what had happened.

Penny was explaining the situation when Sergeant Ryder arrived. He took over where Penny left off.

There was a witness to the accident who was walking her dog across the street in the park. She said she saw the truck come racing around the corner and directly into the front of Quinn's jeep. She confirmed the truck never stopped or hardly slowed as it sped off down the street.

Archer asked if the witness had described the truck. The police officer replied it was a dark colored 4X4 crew cab with lights across the roof. Ryder said an all points bulletin had been issued for the truck.

The doctor appeared and stated Quinn had a possible concussion and would be kept overnight for observation. She had twelve stitches in her chin from a deep cut but was otherwise in pretty good shape.

Archer and Remy debated whether or not to notify Brick. They decided to speak to Quinn about it first.

The doctor said they could see Quinn briefly but could not carry on a conversation. Even the police would have to wait until morning.

The waiting room was full of people, practically the entire alumni committee who were at the club when it happened. They were all relieved to hear Quinn would be okay.

Remy promised to let Penny know the next morning how Quinn was and she would inform everyone else.

In a few minutes Remy, Archer, and Sergeant Ryder were the only ones left in the waiting room.

"Was this an accident Sergeant, or was it intentional?" Archer asked. "For some reason I don't think it was just a random thing. Quinn's been investigating this old murder case and I'm wondering if this had anything to do with it." Archer was very angry over this happening to the daughter he loved like his own.

"Archer, the investigation has just begun. I know you're concerned and I will keep you informed. Don't jump to any conclusions. I will speak with Quinn tomorrow and we'll take it from there. Go home and get some sleep. Quinn is in good hands. We'll talk tomorrow."

With that said, Sergeant Ryder decided to station an officer at the hospital, just as a precaution. He wasn't satisfied it was an accident and wanted to be certain the patient was secure.

Quinn slept most of the night, although not a restful sleep. The nurses were very attentive and made sure she was alert and responsive. She had constant visions of a truck coming straight at her and she tried to turn away from it but it kept coming and coming.

She awoke the next morning with pain in her head and pain underneath her chin. The clock said not even six o'clock. The hospital was abuzz with trays banging and carts being wheeled from room to room. The night shift was leaving and the day shift was coming to work. Her blood had been drawn and her vital signs checked.

She knew someone would be in to question her in a few hours. What could she tell them? It happened so fast. Was it even real or her imagination? Being in a hospital told her it was real. She wasn't kidding herself. It was a warning. She just knew that's what it was. Someone didn't want her pursuing this case. She was warned and now it happened. Her parents would be scared to death. What if they tell Brick? No, please don't even think of doing that! Quinn prayed her parents wouldn't do that.

The doctor came in and checked her over. He said she could go home if she promised to stay in bed and rest for a few days. No driving, no activity for at least a week.

Took appeared along with another police officer. He asked her a million questions, only half she could answer with any real certainty.

"No," she didn't recognize the vehicle. "No," she didn't see the license plate. "No," she didn't see the driver.

"Quinn," said Took. "We have no idea if this was intentional or not. Until we do, I am asking you to put aside this investigation of yours into the murder of your real father. You owe it to your friends, your husband and especially Remy and Archer, to lay low and let us handle it. Now promise me you'll do as I ask."

"I will do as you say for now, Took. If this was an attempt on my life or just a warning, it will only make me more determined to see this case through. It was a cowardly thing to do. Right now I'm feeling lousy but that will change shortly and I will follow through. Right now you have my word."

"Thanks, Quinn. Your parents are waiting to come in so I will leave you alone for now. Come see me in a few days and we'll talk. Take care of yourself and follow the doctor's orders." Took gave her a kiss on her cheek and walked out of the room, nodding to her parents that they could go in and see their daughter.

Remy was the first one in followed by Archer. She rushed over to the bed and stared down at her daughter. "My goodness, Quinn. What would we have done if something happened to you? We love you so much. Just look at you all bruised and looking like you ran over by a truck!"

"Well, gee, thanks for that description, Mom. Now I really feel wonderful." Quinn attempted a smile but it hurt too much and she grimaced with the pain.

"Now look what you did, Remy," Archer said as he bent down to kiss the hurt away. "You're beautiful to me, sweetheart. We're here to take you home and see that you're settled in your apartment. Your mother almost collapsed with fright last night when she saw you lying in the hospital. Please tell us you are finished with this silly search for your dad's killer. We cannot bear another scare like this." Archer took her hand in his huge one and patted it ever so gently.

"I'm sorry guys. I didn't mean to have the accident and frighten everyone. Please, please tell me you didn't call Brick. I implore you not to tell him. He would rush here and cause all kinds of trouble."

"We decided to wait and ask you, baby." Her mother looked at Quinn and then at her husband. "Archer thinks we should call him. After all he is your husband. He would be angry with us if we didn't tell him."

"Double or triple that anger toward me," claimed Quinn. "Let's keep it to ourselves for now. What Brick doesn't know won't hurt him." Or us she thought.

Quinn's jeep was totaled in the crash. She had loved that car. There wasn't a bit of hesitation in deciding she would get another jeep. She chose a fire engine red one with black leather interior. The personalized license plate read *FEDQRSD.* If someone wanted to find her they wouldn't have any trouble. Her parents thought it was a brash and foolish thing to do but Quinn was determined not to let a coward gain control and think their cowardly act had scared her into dropping her investigation.

The scar on her chin was healing. She hoped it would hardly be noticeable by the time of the reunion in just a few weeks.

CHAPTER NINETEEN

Chance Kidder was turning thirteen. His parents were throwing a big family party to celebrate the event. Chance was a miracle child. His parents had tried for years to have a child. When Carrie finally delivered a healthy baby boy the family rejoiced. Chance was born to older parents and was treated like an adult most of his life. He was showered with attention and given every opportunity to excel in school and sports and other endeavors.

He was a great kid. Polite, smart, and eager to learn, he was an exceptional student.

The family adored him. Quinn was looking forward to the party. She knew how much Carrie and Ben had wanted this child. She was glad she was able to attend his party. It was a great way to see members of her family she hadn't seen in many years.

Cindy had called and said she would be coming. She would stay with Ben and Carrie and be there to help with the food and preparations.

Emily was the cake baker. She made beautiful cakes for weddings and other important events. Chance was into basketball so she was planning a cake with a basketball court and a figurine depicting him shooting a foul shot. She had the team colors and his jersey number. He would love it.

The day of the party was sunny and warm. No rain showers were expected. Archer made sure he he'd packed the car with extra lawn chairs so everyone would be comfortable. Remy had made a salad and Quinn volunteered to bring a cooler of drinks.

The party was to begin at one and go until the last person left. In this family that could be an all nighter if people began to play cards or other games.

Ben and Carrie lived in the country. Ben raced go karts in the summer and had a garage with all kinds of engines and racing stuff in it. Chance was his crew chief. The men gathered around the garage when they first arrived to talk shop and pretend they knew all about how to win at car racing.

Chance greeted everyone and directed the women to the kitchen and the men up the hill to the garage. The children who came immediately headed to the games which had been set up in the backyard.

Quinn went directly to the patio and put the cooler alongside the other coolers that held drinks for the thirsty crowd. The patio was already a focal point for many of the attendees. Quinn recognized a few but she spent the next few minutes being introduced to relatives and family friends she hadn't seen in years or never knew at all.

One of the guests was Chance's grandfather, Hank Kidder. Quinn hadn't thought she would see him here. She would never have recognized him. He was older and looked unwell. He had lost a lot of weight and walked very slowly. He certainly wasn't the same man she had pictured who had been tough and menacing. His hair was white and he sat in his chair not talking or being sociable. He barely gave her a passing glance.

Chance came over and offered his grandfather a drink but Hank said, "no he wasn't thirsty at the moment." He thanked Chance and said he wished him a happy birthday. Chance gave him a hug and walked away.

When Remy and Archer brought their chairs to the patio, they both acknowledged Hank's presence with a nod and a short hello. Hank gave a small wave but was silent.

Quinn didn't know if she should introduce herself to the man or not. She continued to watch him to get a sense of his reaction to certain people before approaching him. He seemed to be polite to those who asked about his health and how he was feeling. He ate very little and seemed content just being there for his son and grandson.

Cindy and Emily told him he should eat something and that they would fix him a plate but he just said no, he wasn't hungry.

The food was lined up on three six foot tables. Quinn had never seen so much food in her life. Someone had brought a huge ham. Carrie had made a roaster of pulled pork. Others had brought fried chicken. All kinds of salads and side dishes were displayed including trays of relishes and pots of beans.

Emily's cake was the highlight of the dessert table. There were pies and cakes, cupcakes, and brownies.

Quinn thought she would surely be returning to San Diego at least ten pounds heavier than when she left America's finest city.

Ben had set out four large trash cans so cleanup was easy. Each was lined with a plastic trash bag so when one got full it was removed and another put in its place.

Carrie announced the birthday cake would be cut in a few hours so everyone's food could settle. This was met with a sigh of relief from just about everybody. A few of the smaller children complained but they were assured they could still have a brownie or cupcake.

The party slowly began to quiet down. Older ones dozed in their chairs. Babies were put down for naps in a back bedroom that was lined with playpens and other sleeping apparatus.

Games were set up in the yard and everyone was invited to join in playing volleyball or bocce ball or badminton. There was even a croquet game. Quinn hadn't seen one of those in years. She was tempted to try her hand at playing when she noticed Hank sitting off to one side by himself. This might be the perfect opportunity to ask him some questions. Would he cause a scene? That was a worry. Would he get angry and begin spouting obscenities?

Quinn decided she would take her chances and simply walked up to him and asked if he would mind if she sat down next to him.

He looked at her and shrugged so she pulled a chair up closer to him and sat down.

"I know you don't know me, Mr. Kidder. I am Quinn Reaghan, Remy's daughter." She waited for his reaction.

"I know who you are, honey. I know about your accident and why you are here and all about your investigation." Hank crossed his legs and picked some lint off his slacks.

"Would you mind answering some questions," Quinn asked.

"Believe it or not I would be happy to set the record straight on your father's murder. I am the only one who can. I am a sick old man with nothing to lose by telling the story. It's been inside me for years."

Quinn could not believe what her ears were hearing. She had feared the worst from this man and here he was anxious to tell her everything.

"Thank you for saying that, Mr. Kidder. I was afraid you might be angry with me for bringing the subject up. It's been a long time and I don't want to offend anyone but I need to have some answers about the night my father was killed."

"Ask away, Quinn. I have nothing to hide. It's actually a relief to talk about it."

Hank settled back in his chair and looked her square in the eye and smiled like a Cheshire cat with a bowl of cream in front of it.

Quinn was a bit unsettled by his smirky smile. She knew behind that smile was a man who couldn't be trusted any further than a snake in the grass. She decided to begin with a direct question.

"Mr. Kidder, do you think Grey Falls River's police chief killed Quade Reaghan?"

Hank didn't even blink an eye. "No, John Farraday didn't kill your father. Let me tell you the complete story of how that night went down. Listen to me closely, you are the only one I've ever told it to. Perhaps it's time I tell someone so the truth is known before I kick the bucket."

Quinn wished she had a tablet or something to write down what he was about to reveal to her. She was afraid to step away and get something in case it destroyed the moment and Hank would back down. So she just said okay and sat forward so she wouldn't miss a word of what he was about to say. This was totally awesome she thought. She would have shouted with joy if possible. The last thing she wanted was to draw attention to them over in this corner. She prayed there wouldn't be a distraction.

"First of all, I had nothing against Quade Reaghan. I hardly knew the man. I had no time for your mother. She was despicable to me and to this day I can hardly stand to look at her. I was forced to give her half the money from the bar we owned and I hate her for that among other things." The fury in his voice was unmistakable. Quinn didn't react but she was shaking inside with anger herself at how this man who treated her mother so terribly could have the audacity to say these things to her. She let him continue his tirade.

"I knew what was going down. Quade's wife, Corinne, told me what she had planned. She asked me if I wanted Remy killed too. I said no, I couldn't kill the mother of my children. I had the opportunity to take her out but I didn't. It might have been the only moral thing I have done in my life." Hank bent his head and paused for a brief moment.

"Did you date Corinne? Quinn asked softly. "I mean I heard you visited mom together where she worked a few times and threats were made."

Hank looked at her a minute before replying. "Corinne and I did go out to dinner a few times. She called me, I didn't contact her. I think she did it out of spite. She was obsessed about Quade living with Remy. One night we showed up at the restaurant where your mother worked. Corrine walked right up to your mom and stuck her finger right in her face. She said Remy could have Quade for one year but then she had to let him go, or else there would be severe consequences."

"What did my mother do?" Quinn asked, totally entranced by what this man was saying.

"She didn't respond, she simply turned and walked away. I could tell she was shaken and on the verge of tears but she calmly walked away. We left but you know it was a year and a day from that night that Quade was shot and killed. That coincidence scared me to death when I thought about it later." Hank's voice quavered a little when he made that last statement.

A chill crept over Quinn. That was a real threat that evil woman made to my mother, she thought. "Was Corinne jealous and capable of carrying through with her threat? What I mean by that, was she aggressive and tough enough to shoot Quade?"

"Corinne didn't kill Quade Reaghan. She had him killed. Corinne was a huge gambler. She hung out at the racetrack. The bar she went to with her friend, Josephine Battaglia, had many unsavory characters who hung out there. She told me she hired two of these thugs to take Quade down. That was when she asked me if I wanted to include Remy for another thousand dollars. She told me step by step what was going to happen and how it would go down. I told her I wanted nothing to do with her scheme."

"Why didn't you go to the police and tell them her plans?" Quinn was astounded at what he had just revealed to her.

"I didn't want to be involved. She had been dating John too and who was I to repeat what a mad woman was talking about. I didn't have any proof. I had no names of the men she had met in the bar. I had nothing but a threat made from a distraught crazy woman."

"Where is this bar?"

"It's in a bad area of Buffalo. You wouldn't want to go there. It might not even be there now. There has been some reconstruction in that part of town in recent years. It was called Petrino's at the time, twenty-eight years ago."

"Mr. Kidder, where were you when the murder of my father went down?"

"I was at the bar in Cherrydale with Ben and Cindy. I was there until my night shift began at work here in town. The police showed up and took me down to the station for questioning. I was their prime suspect. Work was miserable from then on. My boss finally gave me two

131

weeks paid time off until things cooled down. Everyone was blaming me and accusing me of being the killer. It was unbearable."

Quinn wasn't about to feel bad about this man's harassment. As far as she was concerned he knew what was going to happen and did absolutely nothing to prevent it. He was as guilty as the trigger man and his accomplice.

"I don't have reason to lie to you, Quinn. I didn't even have to talk to you. This is the truth as I've known it to be. It's time it was known. I've kept it to myself for twenty-eight years. Do with it what you want."

"Mr. Kidder, one last question. Do you think Corinne committed suicide?"

"I will answer that this way. I think the press killed her. The paper reported, she was going to an attorney on Monday and make a statement. She was found dead on Sunday, supposedly by her own hand. She was lying dead in the garage with the car engine running. They said she left a note saying she was responsible for Quade's death. Could she have done this to herself? Anything is possible. I personally think she was murdered to shut her up. That's just my opinion. Corinne was one tough lady. She had a son she was very close to by her first marriage. I don't think she would kill herself out of guilt. She didn't balk at having her husband shot down in cold blood. I doubt if she had a change of heart but we'll never know."

"Did her son kill Quade?"

"No, he wasn't that type. He loved his mother and he didn't like Quade but it wasn't a deep hate. He was actually a quiet kid who went his own way. Unfortunately he died of cancer awhile back."

Hank rose to his feet a bit unsteady. "I'm going home. It's been a bit of a long day for this old man. You have my word on this story. I may be known as a mean son of a bitch, but I didn't kill Quade or anyone else. I told you the truth."

Quinn rose also. She put her hand on Hank Kidder's arm and thanked him for telling her his story. She wished him well and he went into the house to say goodbye to his family.

Quinn immediately went to her car and wrote down everything she could remember of their conversation. It came as quite a revelation to hear this version of what happened. Another new twist in this captivating tale.

Why would someone still be intent on hurting her to keep her from further investigation. She was sure the two unknown hired killers were long gone. Hank as much as said they were out of the area. Twenty-eight years had passed. Surely they were out of the picture. Corinne was dead so they had no reason to fear retribution from her.

The cutting of the cake took place while she was pondering the recent interview. She exited her car and joined the others to help serve the cake and ice cream. Chance was going to open his gifts before heading to another party given by his friends at a lake close by.

It had been an eventful day and Quinn was exhausted by the time she got home. Tomorrow was another day.

CHAPTER TWENTY

Quinn visited the cemetery twice the next week. The first visit was to Corinne Reaghan's grave. Quinn wanted to get a feel toward this woman who anguished in her grief and took her own. Or did she? Was she that distraught? Was her guilt so overwhelming that this was the only out? She had police guard when she was released from her hospital stay. Had she threatened suicide or was it because she was a suspect in her husband's murder?

One of the police officers who had the duty guarding her had said he felt like he was living with a killer. Why had he felt that way? Quinn wondered how the woman could even remain in the home where the murder took place. That didn't seem normal to her. Her death occurred two months after Quade's. Did her horrible deed finally reach her heart and she could no longer live with the knowledge that she was part of a murder scheme?

The fact that she was found incoherent by a neighbor following the shooting suggests it affected her immediately. The bruises on her body could have been caused by the murderer if she had begun screaming and sobbing and was yelling she had done something terrible and needed to confess. Her guilt was so immense that her mind retreated back to a safer place where denial took over.

It seemed strange that she wasn't questioned by someone other than the local police department. Doctors had been present and she was under the care of psychiatrists. Quinn would have loved to see a few of those sealed documents.

"Talk to me," Quinn pleaded. The cold stone just sat there quiet and unrevealing. It didn't give up any secrets from the grave.

Quinn next knelt at the grave of her father. A peace came over her as she prayed at the site. It was as if he knew she was there and was releasing her from her search.

It had been an intense six weeks since she had returned home. She had been given many answers but she knew the search wasn't over. Her heart was still pushing her to do more. She wouldn't find rest until she knew who had pulled the trigger.

What was the next step? Quinn didn't know but she knew whatever it was it would reveal itself in due time.

Two weeks left to solve the mystery. She was sure she was close. Someone out there was afraid. Eventually they would slip and make a mistake. She would be ready when that happened.

CHAPTER TWENTY-ONE

The following week Quinn spoke with an FBI agent who covered the bank armored car robbery the year before Quade's death. Rumor had it that Quade had come across the accident and supposedly stole some of the money which was scattered amid the wreckage.

Would it be easy to pass up a wreck with money lying everywhere and not be tempted to take some? It was on a lonely country road with very little traffic. Would a normal person's conscience say just a little wouldn't hurt. Banks wouldn't miss just a little. One of the guards was dead and the other was badly injured. No one would know.

Somehow Corinne's son knew. He had been in the Army with a man who reported the theft

FROM PRIMARY

TOTAL PURCHASE

ACCOUNT # ***** ***** ***** 0856 S
REF # 234700607946
NETWORK ID. 0074 APPR CODE 302363
TERMINAL # 08002133

12/11/12   20:36:43

ITEMS SOLD 6

TC# 5703 0557 3204 1522 0184

Don't forget -
pick up layaway items by Dec 14
12/11/12   20:36:46

to Corinne's friend. This was after the son's death. He knew the story of the accident and how Quade came across it while on a job-related trip to a nearby town.

The agent told Quinn the money was traced to an account in Corinne's name. He said it wasn't a major amount and the case against her never came to trial because of the subsequent murder and her death.

The media and the police had considered a connection to the Buffalo Mafia but nothing was ever proven. It was concluded that it was simply a tragic accident and not in any way connected to Quade's murder. Still it was difficult to think of her father as a thief. He gave it to his wife willingly or did she say it would be easier for her to put it in an account out of the area so no one would be suspicious. To Quinn that made more sense. Corinne wasn't exactly a saint or upstanding citizen. She would of course reveal this information to her son.

She wondered if her mother knew anything about this incident. Did she receive any of the ill begotten funds? If she had what would Quinn do with the information? Would she look the other way? Maybe it was best to let this one go. Let sleeping dogs lie. Her mother meant too much to her to even ask the question.

Quinn decided to take her parents out to dinner that evening. Her mother needed a break from cooking and her dad needed to get out and enjoy a few hours of relaxation. He had been at the Elks every night working on the float for the upcoming parade.

There was a delightful restaurant on the lake about thirty miles away. The drive would be scenic and restful and they could chat along the way. They even came across a roadside produce stand which gave Remy many happy moments choosing fresh peaches and veggies.

The restaurant wasn't overly crowded and they captured a table overlooking the pretty lake. They watched water skiers and boating enthusiasts sail by waving at the restaurant guests as they flew by. Archer ordered an array of appetizers and drinks for everyone. It was such a relaxing evening and her parents appreciated Quinn's treat.

Quinn was anxious to get home and call Brick. She felt like talking things out with him and especially hearing his voice. She needed the comfort of his arms but that wasn't possible so she would take the next best thing. She wouldn't have to share all that was going on in her life at the moment but just talking to him would clear her mind.

As Archer was turning the corner onto their street they could see fire trucks and police cars with flashing lights parked in front of their house. The neighbors were all out in the street and kids and dogs were running amok through the neighborhood, apparently excited over all the commotion.

Archer stopped the car and immediately ran toward the house and the nearest police officer he could find. Quinn helped her mother out of the car before taking her elbow and helping her cross the fire hoses lining the driveway.

Archer had found Ben inside the house and now they were both walking toward Quinn and her mother who were almost entering the front door.

"Archer, what on earth has happened," Remy began, reaching out to grab his arm. "Ben, what are you doing here, honey? Are you okay?" She looked him up and down as only a mother would at a time like this.

"I'm fine mom. You'd better sit down so I can explain everything. It's a minor emergency. Don't worry." He glanced over at Quinn and raised his eyebrows as he was leading his mother to the sofa. "You just stay here and I'll be back in a minute. Don't get up as you'll just be in the way of the emergency personnel. Archer, get mom some coffee or something and stay with her until I get back. Quinn, come with me a minute."

Quinn followed Ben into the garage. The smell of smoke was almost overbearing. All the doors were open so it was getting better. Still, Quinn began coughing so Ben ushered her out to the backyard.

"What's going on, Ben?" Quinn asked, all the while wiping her eyes and nose to clear the smoke from them.

"I came over to bring mom some stuff Carrie had canned. I came into the kitchen and noticed the door into the garage was open so I went over to close it and saw a man run out the back door of the garage. I went to chase after him but smelled smoke so I called 911 and the rest you know."

"Where and how did the fire start?" Quinn asked.

"We are waiting for the fire marshal to arrive. It appears the fire started from an incendiary device placed under the stairs to your apartment. Took is upstairs now checking things out up there. I personally think your last incident and this one are connected. What do you think?" Ben sat down on one of the patio benches and motioned for Quinn to do the same.

Quinn started for the stairs but Ben grabbed her arm and pulled her down beside him. "Let's wait a few minutes and Took will find us and tell us what he knows. You can't just go running off, not knowing if the guy planted anything in your apartment or your car. It happened once, it can happen again. This is getting serious, Quinn. Next time it could even be worse."

Quinn knew he was telling the truth. What would happen the next time. Could she put her family in jeopardy over this pursuit of her father's killer?

Took Ryder strode out to the patio with a concerned look on his face. "We didn't find anything unusual in your apartment, Quinn, but I would prefer you stay elsewhere for a few days just in case we missed something. I don't know what's going on but it's not good. I'm bringing in the State Fire Marshal to check things out. We're not going to mess around with this."

Sergeant Ryder stood in front of Quinn, his legs spread wide and his arms folded over his chest. "I want you to listen to me, young lady," he began while making certain he had her full attention.

"This craziness has got to stop. Right now. This very minute. If I hear of one more incident, I will personally put you on the next plane back to San Diego. Not only that but I will call your husband and tell him to meet your plane and make sure you stay three thousand miles away from Grey Falls River!

Furthermore, you have two weeks left in my town and I don't want to hear even one word of anything related to Quade Reaghan's murder. Do we understand each other Quinn?"

"Good Lord, Took," Quinn began, It's not that big a deal! I understand this is strange and unusual but . . ."

Took interrupted her with a look that even made Ben take a step back.

"Enough! You will not try to pretend this is nothing but a small incident. It's damn serious and who knows how many lives are endangered with all this investigation. You are not a police officer. You are a United States Federal Prosecutor. An attempt on your life is serious business. You are putting yourself, your family, my office, and this town in a precarious position. There will be no more!"

Took turned and walked into the house to see how her parents were doing and tell them the exact same thing. He wanted to assure them he had taken care of things.

Quinn stood in the backyard looking at the sky as if pondering what her next step would be. Should she just pack up now and head back to San Diego? Maybe that would be the best thing. She had certainly made a mess of this investigation. It wasn't her intention to bring harm to her parents or cause them concern for her safety.

Ben came up behind her and put his hands on her shoulders. "It's okay, little sis, I promise it will be okay. Just let it go. You know your dad wouldn't want anything to happen to you over a crime that was committed twenty-eight years ago. Mom and Archer could have lost their house tonight."

"I know, Ben. I can't stop thinking about that. It's just I'm so close to solving this thing. The killer has shown he's afraid. He knows

I'm closing in. I can feel his presence. I will slow things down. Maybe I will even go home. I won't let anyone else be hurt."

Quinn turned and headed back into the garage. The firemen were wrapping up their time there and heading back to the station. She saw Took getting into his car and talking on his phone.

Archer was checking out the damage to his garage. The fire chief was explaining to him what had happened and she heard him say the State Fire Marshal would be there soon. Archer thanked him and his department for taking care of things so quickly and sparing his home.

Ben went into the house to check on his mother before heading home. He had been waiting to see if Quinn would ask him if he recognized the man running from the scene. He knew she wouldn't think it was his father. The man could barely walk, let alone run the way that guy did. Well, the guy actually lumbered rather than sprinted. Ben thought he could have caught the guy if the smell of

147

smoke hadn't stopped him. He hoped this would be the end of it. Quinn had made this town sit up and take notice, if nothing else. He chuckled at the thought of her shaking up some of its important citizens. His little sister had chutzpah. He liked that.

When Quinn finally went into the house she found her mother upstairs making up the bed in her old bedroom.

"Mom, I'm sorry, so sorry for what happened tonight. I wouldn't hurt you and dad for all the world. I promise I'll just pack my things and go home. I should never have started this business in the first place. I was just so sure I could do it."

"Oh honey," her mother began, "I'm not blaming you for what happened. It just makes me so angry someone could do this to us. If it's someone I know in this town, I will gladly see them punished to the full extent of the law!" Remy sat down on the bed and drew Quinn to her. "Let's just sleep on it and discuss it tomorrow when we're both rested."

CHAPTER TWENTY-TWO

Quinn awoke to the sounds of thunder and the flashing of lightning outside her window. She had spent a restless night going back and forth over the events of the night before. Someone was definitely trying to get rid of her or at least discourage her efforts to pursue the case.

She could smell breakfast being prepared downstairs. She hurriedly took a shower and got dressed.

Her parents were enjoying a cup of coffee and chatting about their plans for the day when she entered the kitchen. Quinn loved that farmhouse kitchen. It was quite large. Remy had painted it a bright yellow with a border of light blue featuring various kinds of songbirds. It was a bright and cheerful room dominated by a large round maple table in the center.

Remy had set the table with blue and white dishes on yellow placemats. It just looked so inviting this morning.

Quinn remarked about the work her mother had gone to make the morning special.

"Your father and I decided we would go on with our lives and not let last night change us in any way. So, honey, you just set yourself right down and let's have a nice breakfast and make some plans for the rest of your stay." She gave Quinn a hug and pulled a chair out for her.

After breakfast, Quinn went upstairs and made her bed. Her parents had not wanted to discuss the fire at all and had insisted she stay until her reunion and planned departure date. They understood the stand Took had taken about her investigation and agreed one-hundred percent that she should just put it aside and move on with her life. Nothing good would come of continuing the search.

Quinn thought they all had their heads in the sand but didn't argue or disagree. She knew you just couldn't stop and throw your hands up in the air and give up. There had been a murder. That was real. There was no statute of limitations on murder. Because of the two incidents that had happened, it was now a fact that someone in Grey Falls River was involved and wanted her gone.

She would keep a low profile and not discuss her findings with anyone.

Later that morning when she knew Brick would be at his desk she gave him a call. He said it was bright and sunny in Los Angeles. He sounded happy to hear from her. He asked about her parents and about how the plans for her reunion were going.

The conversation was light and pleasant. He was anxious to see her and told her about a case he was working on that involved a professor they had in law school and one of his students that had been found murdered. Apparently, the young student had been thrown off a cliff near Malibu Canyon. She had the professor's name and home phone number in her pocket. Brick thought it would prove easy to solve with all the evidence they had collected.

Quinn kept the conversation going by listening and commenting occasionally on what he was talking about.

"Quinn, I am sensing you have something else on your mind this morning. What's wrong?"

Quinn thought she had been speaking in a normal tone but Brick knew her too well.

"I'm fine. I've been here six weeks and I suppose maybe I'm a little homesick," she responded with a little catch in her voice that she hadn't planned on.

"Sweetheart, I sense a bit of sadness in your voice. Do you want me to come there?"

"No, Brick, I can get through the next few weeks. I'm just feeling a bit melancholy this morning. It's a dreary day and I am thinking of you in sunny California and your busy social life and busy work schedule. I guess I'm ready to go home. I miss you, I really do."

Brick had to pause at that statement and smile to himself. "You don't how happy that makes me to hear you say that Quinn. It's all I can do to not leap up from this desk and head to LAX and fly there this instant. You know how I feel about you, sweetie."

"Oh, Brick, it's just a passing thing. I'll be fine. I will see you soon and we'll swap stories. Get busy on your case and don't worry anymore about me. I'm going to bounce right back to my cheerful self and go bake some cookies while mom's at a meeting of her bridge club. Thanks for talking to me. I feel much better now."

"Okay, darlin. Wish I was there to have a cookie or two. Take care of yourself. Hug your mom for me and give Archer a big hello. Call me anytime. I love you."

"I love you too, Brick, I really do. Bye."

Quinn didn't know if she was content to end their conversation but she did feel better. She was assured that Brick hadn't found out what was going on in Grey Falls River. Apparently Sergeant Ryder hadn't let that cat out of the bag. She would have to be very careful from this point on.

Brick sat in his chair reviewing the phone call word by word. Quinn was keeping something from him. He sensed her need to talk but she definitely was not on the up and up. He could always tell when she was keeping something from him. Her voice always dropped a few octaves and there would be a catch to it. He'd been putting off his trip but maybe he should make the effort to fly east and see what was going on with his wife.

CHAPTER TWENTY-THREE

Penny and Quinn were on their way to the mall to do some shopping for decorations for the reunion. Nothing too garish, just some balloons and maybe some gossamer for across the ceiling.

Penny was trying to get her friend's mind off the recent attempts on her life. Quinn seemed to not be affected by them but Penny knew she was feeling the strain. Quinn had become tired and distracted. She stayed at home and only ventured out to go grocery shopping with her mother or to dinner with both parents.

The party store always lifted one's spirits. Everything in it shouted happy times. Quinn suggested brightly colored balloons instead of the same old school colors. She wanted matching tablecloths and paper goods too. By the time they exited the store both their arms were full of fun stuff. Penny was happy to see Quinn with a smile on her face and actually looking forward to their upcoming event.

The decided to have lunch at a Mexican restaurant they came across. Quinn remarked she had been hungry for Mexican food. She loved it. Of course San Diego was a haven for good food, especially Mexican. Penny wasn't sure she would like it but she ended up eating hers and sampling Quinn's too.

That evening Quinn asked Penny if she would go with her to the bar outside of town where her mother had worked when she was living with Quade. At first Penny refused, reiterating what Sergeant Ryder had told Quinn about doing anymore investigating.

"Penny, we're just going to see what the place is like. I know there have been some changes but things around here don't change that much. I just want to get a feel of the place where Corinne made all her threats against my mother and Quade."

"I don't believe you really want to do this. I really can't believe I am going to do this!" said Penny as she walked out the door and got back into Quinn's jeep.

"Atta girl," quipped Quinn as she hopped into the driver's seat. "Let's go on an adventure. Just like the old days, right girlfriend?"

"Yeah, well there hadn't better be any problems or Took will throw me out of town too," Penny laughed.

The bar was actually a restaurant too. It had a pool table and an old juke box. The floors were wooden and the interior looked like it had seen better times. The bar was old and the stools were a mismatch of colors and styles.

There was a band playing country music and a few couples were on the dance floor doing more of a struggle to stay upright than truly dancing.

Both women were skeptical about taking a seat anywhere. They certainly the center of attention. Anybody new was a reason to almost stop the music and make an announcement. This was just the way local bars were. Quinn wasn't surprised. Penny was afraid she would be recognized and the rumors would fly all around town.

"Let's just order a drink and act like we're just here for a quick one and then we'll leave," Quinn whispered. "Just act casual and like we do this all the time."

"Right," replied Penny. "Like I always hang out in dives like this. Oh, Oh, here comes a local cowboy heading this way. You handle this."

"You ladies want a drink," the biker dude asked, trying his best to appear somewhat presentable. His breath about knocked both the girls right out of the booth.

"Thank you, kind sir, but my friend and I have our drinks and then we're headed back out on the road. Thank you for your kind offer."

Quinn didn't want to offend the guy so she answered him the best way she could think would dismiss his advances.

"Okay my ladies, maybe next time," he slurred as he walked back to his buddies swaying to remain on his feet.

"I think we should just leave," whispered Penny as she began to collect her purse from the seat next to her.

"Now Penny, don't get too impatient. That one guy at the bar acts like he's been here forever. I think I'll ask him a few questions before we leave. Maybe he's been coming here for years. He just might remember my mother working here. Just let me ask."

"Oh no, here we go," thought Penny as Quinn got up and walked over to the bar.

"Excuse me sir but have you been coming here a long time? You look like you know your way around and you seem to know everyone who walks through the door."

The old man looked Quinn up and down before replying. "I've been coming here for over forty years, young lady. What is it you're looking for?"

"I was wondering if you might remember a waitress here back in the eighties. She was a short, petite gal. Dark hair and a quick smile. Her name was Remy."

"Remy Kidder?" The old man slapped his knee and took a long swig of his beer. "Everybody knew Remy. She was the best waitress they ever had here. Certainly, the friendliest. Why do you ask about her?"

"I'm doing a story on her and a guy she dated who was killed back in nineteen eighty four. I understand he came in here with her a few times and so did his wife. I'm just looking for information and thought you might be able to help." Quinn signaled the bartender to bring her new friend another beer. A loose tongue tells more stories than a sober one.

"I don't remember much about Remy's personal life but I do know her ex husband came in a few times and they had a few words. He was a mean drunk and always had to be asked to leave. In fact, I threw his ass out of here one night. She really liked this one boyfriend who came in here a lot and waited for her shift to end. I think he's the one you're talking about. She quit right after he was killed. He was a good looking guy, looked like Mickey Mantle back in his younger days."

Quinn wanted to keep him talking so she kept refilling his glass. Penny kept motioning her to leave but she was on a hot streak now and wasn't about to stop.

"Did anything ever turn violent?" Quinn asked him, while turning down a drink sent over by one of the patrons.

"One night this guy came in and began picking a fight. This guy, Mickey Mantle, told him to shut up and get lost but this guy kept badgering him. Finally, the two started throwing punches and ended up in the parking lot. Remy's friend beat the living crap out of this guy who started it. I heard later that he was the chief of police in Grey Falls River."

Quinn almost fell off the bar stool. She asked if he was sure about that and he swore it was the truth. This was news! Big news!

She thanked him for talking to her. He said anytime he could swap stories with a pretty girl made his day.

Penny came over and met her half way out of the bar. She could tell Quinn was excited just by the look on her face.

"Don't tell me, the old fart actually knew something!" she fairly shrieked.

"Shush, Penny. I'll tell you all about it when we're safely in the car and heading home. This isn't the best place to be carrying on a conversation!"

"Oh really, Quinn? You leave me by myself in a pickup bar out in the middle of nowhere and now you tell me this isn't the best place to have a conversation! Give me a break!"

"I'm sorry about leaving you, Penny. You won't believe what this guy said. He knew my mother and he knew my father too. What a coincidence, don't you think? I am so psyched." Quinn fairly danced her way to the car.

The way home was quick because the time passed so swiftly. Quinn was all excited about the story she had just heard. Penny began to fear that now Quinn was reenergized and the investigation would begin anew. Just when things were settling down.

"Quinn, you know you promised you would drop this thing. Now here you are, ready to take on the world again. Even I'm tempted to give Brick a call and get him back here."

"No, Penny, I promise I won't go off half-cocked. This is great news though. I will be doing some thinking and maybe a bit of digging to see what I might find. Don't worry, I'll be keeping a low profile. Hey, thanks for going with me, Penny. You're a real trooper." Quinn walked her friend to her car and gave her a hug. "I'll see you when we begin decorating. I can't wait. It's going to be a wonderful time."

Quinn's parents had already retired for the night so she grabbed a glass of milk and a few cookies and went up to her room. She was way too antsy to sleep. Imagine that! Her real dad had beaten up the chief of police. He must have been a real jerk. She had heard Quade had a temper when he became angry. This John Farraday must have had some reason to pick a fight. Perhaps it was true that Corinne and he had a thing going on.

Her mother was probably present when this fight took place. She had never told Quinn about it. She knew her mother didn't want her asking any more questions but this story was too good to just let it slip by. Her mother would be appalled that she had gone to this bar. That wouldn't be a good idea to bring that up.

Finally, around three in the morning, Quinn fell into a fitful sleep. She dreamed about a fair haired handsome man beating up on a bigger man who was nothing but a bully. His face frightened Quinn and yet she had never seen the man in her life. It was pure evil.

CHAPTER TWENTY-FOUR

Archer Morrison was worried about his wife and daughter. He loved Quinn like she was his own flesh and blood. He often wished that were true. This business with investigating the death of her real father left him cold. Yeah, he understood her curiosity and determination. That was the way she was. She was intense. When she was a little girl she would stand square in the middle of a room, cross her arms, and set her mouth and whatever you wanted her to do that she didn't want to do, well. You might as well forget it.

Archer smiled thinking about those days so long ago. What a rascal she was but oh so dear to his heart.

Remy was working as a waitress and bartender when he met her twenty-five years ago. He just happened to stop in the restaurant one night after work to have a cold drink. She was working the bar that evening because the usual bartender had called in sick.

He noticed her smile and easy way of talking right away. She came right over and asked him what his pleasure was. He smiled at that and she laughed. She brought him his cold beer and they chatted awhile. She said she hadn't seen him in the bar before so he explained that he was on a job in that part of the county and just happened by.

By the time he left the bar he had two more beers and stayed for dinner as well. He had also wrangled a date with the pretty waitress.

He was divorced at the time. After being married for twenty years his wife ran off with another man. One of his best friends, in fact. That was a blow to his ego and also the loss of a friend. He had three children at the time and he retained custody as his ex-wife simply wanted her freedom. They were all teenagers. It wasn't easy being left in charge of three teenagers. He had to work full-time and it wasn't always fun to go home and cook dinner and do laundry. He came to respect a woman's place in the home within just a few weeks.

Remy had told him the story of Quade's death in detail so he was made aware early on that she had a small daughter by this man who never knew a baby was on the way. That was sad. It was a gift to him as far as Archer was concerned. A precious gift he treasured to this day.

He never met Quade as far as he knew. He must have been a good man because Remy spoke of him in almost reverent tones.

Archer thought it was a senseless killing. He might have thought or wished his ex-wife was dead but that was a normal thing to do under the circumstances. Normal people just don't go ahead and kill them.

He didn't know Corinne either but she must have been a piece of work.

Now Quinn is here on vacation and all she thinks about is finding out who murdered her biological father. Someone out there knows something because the whole family has been affected by these recent incidents. Although Archer loved Quinn very much, he wished things were back to normal. He and Remy were getting too old to have this interruption in their lives.

He almost called Brick a number of times but knew Quinn did not want her husband to know what was going on in Grey Falls River. If something were to go wrong and Quinn was hurt, the shit would really hit the fan. Not only would Brick be devastated but his anger would be unleashed on everyone who didn't give him a heads up on what was going on.

Just a week to go, he thought. Surely we can make it through seven more days and Quinn would return to her job and home in San Diego and this whole episode would go away, forgotten maybe until her next visit to Grey Falls River.

CHAPTER TWENTY-FIVE

One more week, thought Quinn as she awoke on Monday morning. One week left to solve this case or leave town before it was done. She couldn't continue to work on it once she was home and back to work. She barely had time to think with her caseload in federal court.

She had formed ideas and maybes in her mind but it was mostly speculation. There were so many stories and suspects. If the case had been handled by law enforcement other than the small and less efficient Grey Falls Police Department, it probably could have easily been solved within days.

She had virtually no forensics to fall back on and even less material evidence. A lot was hearsay from individuals who just knew who had done it. Everyone, from the police chief to close friends, to an ex-husband, to a family member, to out of town thugs. One crazy person even suggested Remy did it. It's no wonder some cases go unsolved forever, Quinn thought.

One thing she did know was that the son was dead, the close friend was dead, who knows where the supposed thugs disappeared to, her mother was totally innocent, and the chief of police left town and was probably too embarrassed to show his face in this town again. His ineptitude was a disgrace to law enforcement everywhere.

Archer and her mom were finishing decorating the float for the Elks Club. Quinn had promised she would work on her class float this week. She didn't want to ride on it but she would help them put it together. Saturday morning she would be decorating the hall for the evening's dinner dance.

Quinn was anxious to get home and resume her normal routine. She was clearly ready to focus on her relationship with Brick. If anything, these two months away had been a real eye opener for her as far as how tenuous life was. She wanted a home and family and she just couldn't imagine that without Brick.

He had changed too. She heard it in his words when they spoke and read between the lines when he texted her. They were both ready to move forward with the marriage and make it work.

The class float was being put together in a barn owned by one of Quinn's classmates. Because it was a bicentennial celebration, the class theme was "Taming the Wilderness." Several on the float were dressing like colonial times. Some were woodsmen, some Indians, and others were fur traders and townspeople.

The float had real pine trees, a real log cabin, animals, and even a real waterfall. It promised to be spectacular and a sure first-place winner.

Everyone was in high spirits as they worked together pounding and painting and setting things in place.

Quinn was surprised to see Took arrive in jeans and a tee shirt ready to help. She hadn't seen him since that night of the fire. She wondered if he was still upset with her but he walked right up to her and gave her a hug and asked if she was keeping out of trouble.

"Oh yes, I have been minding my own business, just like you asked," she commented, giving him a hug back.

"That's what I wanted to hear. Let's see what I can do to save this poor excuse for a float," he quipped as everyone began tossing paint brushes and other debris at him.

Thunderclouds began forming in late afternoon so everyone began picking and cleaning up their tools and prepared to close the float safely in the barn.

Quinn thought it was a good feeling to have worked all day on a project other than the law. Laughing and chatting with old friends was so cathartic. Even though she hadn't seen most of these people in ten years, it seemed like yesterday. She hoped it would always be that way.

Emily had invited her to a corn roast that evening so she hurried home to shower and change before heading to the country. Her parents would be joining them in a few hours. She wanted to go early and spend time with her sister.

CHAPTER TWENTY-SIX

The next day was spent organizing her apartment. There was still a faint smell of smoke from the recent fire in the garage. Quinn didn't see anything out of place so if the intruder had been in the apartment it wasn't too apparent.

She gathered her laundry and took care of that first. She checked out her dress she was wearing to the dinner dance. Thankfully it didn't have a smoky odor.

The next step was to drag her suitcase from the closet. She figured she might as well begin packing the stuff she wouldn't be wearing the rest of the week.

When she opened the lid of the suitcase there was a piece of paper taped to the zipper compartment. Quinn sat down on the edge of the bed and waited a moment before opening the folded note. Her mind was smoldering by the time she finished reading the contents. ha, *you didn't catch me this time, you stupid bitch. go back where you came from. your dad was a bastard and i took care of him just like i plan to take care of you and your family. you should never have come back to grey falls river. so long for now . . . i'm watching you!!!*

There was a crude drawing underneath the note. Quinn shivered but not from being cold. It was over eighty degrees outside. How dare this evil person go through her things and leave this stupid note like the coward they were. She was burning with fury at the audacity of it all.

She knew she should take it to the police and have it analyzed. She was consumed with hatred that someone would do this. Now she was shaking with anger and determined to find out who had invaded her personal space and pawed through her closet with their dirty hands.

Quinn paced back and forth until she was exhausted. "Bring it on you brainless twit!" she shouted to the walls. "I'm here, come and give it your best shot, you spineless coward."

She was shouting so loud her mother's dog began to bark inside the house.

After awhile she composed herself and decided to do the right thing. She put the note in her purse, careful not to handle it more than necessary so she wouldn't destroy any forensics on it.

She drove straight to the police station and gave it to Sergeant Ryder. He was astounded that someone had actually been inside her apartment. He and another officer had gone through her place that same night and hadn't found a thing that would suggest a break-in.

"I will send this over to the lab immediately, Quinn. I don't want you worrying or looking over your shoulder every second until you leave. Just be aware and be careful. I'll see that one of my men cruise by your parent's house at least once an hour. This is a genuine threat against you and members of your family. I do not take this lightly. Believe me, it's not just some frivolous joke. You've started something and whoever this is, you're in danger. If I had an ounce of common sense, I would order you to leave Grey Falls River ASAP." Took made a few phone calls and then turned back to Quinn.

"I don't suppose you will take my advice and leave town today?"

"No, I'm not leaving until next Monday at 10 a.m. Let this coward show his face and make an attempt at me or my family and I'll put them away for the rest of their pitiful life."

"That's easy to spout off, Q, but this isn't something that could be solved so easily. Someone could get hurt, even killed. I will agree to let you stay but I'm assigning an officer to you 24/7." He held up his hand when he saw her about to interrupt him. "It's this way or nothing, Quinn."

"I can take care of myself, Took," Quinn sputtered. "I certainly don't need to take up the time of an officer you need for other police work." When Took began to protest, she stopped him with a move that even he didn't see coming. All at once he was on the floor in a stranglehold, her knee in his back and him unable to move.

"I'll let you up when you agree I can continue on as normal. No police escort. Agree?"

"Damn, Quinn, where did you learn to do that?" Took asked as he slowly got up, shaking his head and rubbing his neck.

"I'm married to a police officer, remember? He taught me some moves, just in case. In my line of work I need to be able to protect myself. I'm sorry if I hurt you or got your clean uniform mussed. That would be a bummer," she mused as she brushed him off.

"I'll compromise," Took said as he straightened his belt and fixed his collar. "You never go anywhere unless it's a public place. You let me know where you'll be and who you're with. At night I'll assign an unmarked police car to park by your house."

"Okay, you win this one," Quinn remarked. "I didn't plan on causing a problem, Took. I do apologize for all of this. I'm really surprised this person has been so threatened by my efforts. I really thought it was fruitless. I will be observant and very careful. Thanks for your understanding and your help. You've been a good friend. Thanks."

Quinn gave him a hug and left his office with a promise that he would get back to her on any findings from the note.

Not knowing what else to do, she drove straight home and continued her packing. Her parents called a little after three o'clock and asked her to meet them for an early dinner with her grandmother. That sounded safe enough. She made sure she did the deadbolt on her door before leaving the house. Every light was left on inside and outside. She realized she was being a bit paranoid but that's what one little threatening note could do to the normal person. She was cautious. She would do as Took requested. For once she was sincerely frightened. This was for real.

CHAPTER TWENTY-SEVEN

The rest of the week went according to plan. The float was almost finished. Remy and Archer had a few last minute details to take care of on their float. The real trees had to be put on the floats right before the parade. It wouldn't do to have droopy dead trees for a forest setting.

Quinn had cautioned her parents to be diligent when they went to bed or left for the day. Keep those doors locked and always leave a light or two on. Her mother was a bit intimidated by all this precautionary talk but Quinn assured her it was just common sense. Living in a city Quinn was used to locking doors but here in Grey Falls River, it was easy and common to just walk out of your house and never think of locking your home. Why, what if a neighbor needed a cup of sugar or a tool or their phone wasn't working? It was a different world these days, she explained to Remy. You just don't do that.

One time when she was living in Los Angeles, Quinn stopped for gas at night. The gas station was on a busy street. It was well lighted and there were other cars getting gas. She had reached into her purse to get her gas card when all of a sudden the passenger door opened and before Quinn could react, a black man in a hooded sweatshirt was holding a gun on her and demanded money. He grabbed what she gave him, jumped out of the car, and ran down the street before Quinn could even react. She had sat there totally stunned before a stranger who had witnessed the whole thing, leaned in and asked her if everything was okay.

She had finally answered that yes she was, just a bit shaken by the experience.

Brick had been so upset when he heard about it that he forbade her to ever stop anywhere at night. She was told to always have gas in her car and never let it get below a quarter tank. She had kept that promise and to this day she never let the gas get low. There again, she told her mother, a little common sense can save your life.

Quinn would glance out her upstairs window at night and study the unmarked car sitting on the street a few houses away. She had a .38 caliber pistol sitting on her night stand. She was confident she could use it if someone attempted to enter her apartment uninvited.

Brick had given her one just like it when they were first married. He insisted she go to the shooting range and learn to use it. He was often gone and she was alone at night. She had never had to use it but she at least knew how to load it and shoot straight.

Took had loaned her this gun once he was confident she knew what she doing. He prayed she wouldn't need it. He remarked to his wife that work just wasn't routine since Quinn Reaghan had come to town.

Grey Falls River had been in existence for 200 years. That was a huge reason to celebrate and the town fathers were doing just that. Excitement filled the air as the event planners began setting up booths and vendors filled the city park. The alumni gathering was just a small part of the planned activities. There was a carnival, an art show, the antique car rally, and reenactment of a revolutionary war battle.

The daily paper had new pictures everyday of the preparation for the parade on Saturday. Those who weren't part of the parade were urged to set up their chairs on Friday evening along the parade route. Children were cautioned to stay behind the yellow lines and not run into the street to retrieve candy thrown from the various floats and entrants. That never worked but it was worth the warning.

The weather forecast was for sunny and warm through the weekend. That was a godsend after all the planning that had been in the works for over two years.

It was decided Quinn would meet members of the decorating committee at nine in the morning at the hall where the dinner dance was to be held.

Once the gossamer was draped across the ceiling, the men couldn't get the lights to work. Someone was assigned the task of locating an electrician. Quinn was in the process of handing a screwdriver to a classmate on a ladder when her cell phone buzzed. She walked outside to take the call. Archer said they were about to get on the float to take it to the origination point and her mother wasn't there. She had gone home to pick up the hat he was to wear in the parade. He wondered if Quinn could check on her mother as he had to get the float over to the school. The parade would be starting in less than an hour.

Quinn was only a few blocks from home so she assured her dad that she would take a minute and check on Remy.

Knowing her mother, she probably lost track of time and found something else that grabbed her attention. Quinn explained to her friends that she would be right back. They told her not to hurry, everything was under control.

Remy's car was in the driveway. That was a good sign. At least she knew where her mother was. Quinn went into the house calling her mother's name. No answer. She went upstairs, no mother there. She went into the kitchen, nope, no mom there either. Just one more place to look, the garage.

Quinn opened the door leading into the garage. The first thing she saw was a shotgun being held to her mother's head. Her mother's face was frozen in fear. Holding the shotgun was a huge man, uglier than sin with pure evil in his eyes. The devil himself was Quinn's first thought.

"I was hoping you'd come," the monster said, venom dripping from his snarling mouth. "I thought it was you coming home but it was this pretty little lady here instead. I should have whacked her twenty-eight years ago too but I guess my heart was softer then."

"Mom, are you okay? Has he hurt you," Quinn said quietly staring at her mother and again at the gun so close to her head.

"I'm fine so far," her mother said, trying to make light of a situation that certainly wasn't light. Shaking like a frightened child she could barely stand still but the monster kept pulling her straight up keeping the gun pointed directly at her.

"Shut up the both of you and get into the truck."

Quinn hadn't noticed the large black truck sitting in the garage. She gasped as she recognized the huge machine that had run into her a few weeks before. It had a huge grille on the front. Yes, there was a dent in it that had been caused by the accident.

"So you recognize my truck, do you," snarled the despicable man holding her mother hostage. "It didn't do the job the first time around so let's just see if it can handle the job this time." He shoved her mother toward the truck but Quinn jumped in front of him and reached up to knock the shotgun away from her mother. That move didn't work as the big guy drew back his left arm and knocked Quinn across the garage where she landed on her backside and slammed her head into the wall.

"Listen to me missy. We're all going to get into the truck nice and slow and easy. We're going to take a nice ride into the country. You be nice to me and co-operate and your mother won't be hurt."

"Who are you and why are you doing this to my mother," Quinn demanded as she got to her feet holding her head. She was trying to delay as much as possible. Surely her dad would be worried sick by this time and come looking for them. "If you want to get rid of me, that's one thing, but my mother hasn't done a thing to you. Let her go and I'll go with you quietly."

"I don't think so, young lady. You see, she knows who I am. We're old classmates. She wouldn't give me the time of day when we were in school. Maybe she'll pay attention to me now," he said as he inched his face closer to her mother with a sneer on his ugly face.

Now it became clear to Quinn who this monster was. John Farraday, the old police chief. "Okay, John," she said, trying to make the situation a bit calmer, "I know who you are now. We all know why you're here and what your intentions are. Am I right? You killed my dad and now you plan to kill us too?"

When Quinn fell to the floor her phone had fallen out of her pocket. She had turned while getting to her feet and had snapped a picture of him while he was holding the shotgun to her mother's head. If all else failed at least the police would find her phone and discover who their killer was. She then kicked the phone away so he wouldn't notice it after she was on her feet.

"Tell me, John, is that the same gun that was used to kill my father?" She was trying desperately to buy some time.

"Oh, you noticed, huh? Yeah, I thought it would be a nostalgic touch, using the same shotgun. I didn't kill your father, a couple of hired goons did that. I just made double sure the son of a bitch was good and dead. I delivered the final shot."

Quinn tried to keep her composure. "What about his wife. Did you kill her too?"

John Farraday chuckled and shook his head "she fell apart, the dumb bitch. Here she was all pumped up to kill him and then when the deed was done she began screaming and fighting me. I had to give her a couple of knocks to get her off me. Crazy woman! I couldn't get her to listen to reason when things died down so I had to give her a pill in her coffee to make her drowsy. She had a peaceful death, sleeping like a baby."

"Is that why you left town, John? You hadn't solved the crime. You didn't let any of the other agencies help you? Were they getting suspicious? Maybe they were closing in on you? You weren't exactly the most beloved police chief. I heard you were as crooked as they come. Is that true, Chief Farraday," and she spat in his face.

"That's it, you stupid ass bitch, get in the truck now!" he screamed as she backed away from him.

"No, John," she said very quietly, almost whispering. "No, we are not going to get in your truck. No, we are not going anywhere. If you intend to kill us, it will be done here, right now. Get it over with and be done."

Poor Remy was almost to the point of collapsing in fear. What was Quinn doing? This man would kill them both without a second of remorse. She began to cry.

"I'll show you what's going to happen if you don't get into that truck right now," shouted the man and he took the butt of the shotgun and hit her mother across the face with it and she fell to the floor unconscious.

Quinn had never felt such rage. She took the screwdriver she had put in her jacket when she had gotten the phone call from Archer and without thinking about it at all she raised up and plunged the entire tool into the neck of John Farraday. With a dazed look in his eyes he dropped to the floor deader than a doornail.

She dropped to her knees and held her mother's head in her lap. "Mom," she cried. "Mom, are you okay, speak to me mom," she pleaded, tears streaming down her face. Her mother's face was bleeding and had begun to swell, her nose was broken.

""Quinny, is that you, honey?" her mother whispered.

"Thank God, momma, you're alive," cried Quinn. "Hang in there, we're getting help!" she gently placed her mother on the garage floor and ran over to pick up her phone. She called 911 and asked that the state police come to assist.

Archer could not get off the float once the parade began. He searched the crowd lining the streets thinking Remy would surely be there. He had tried to call the house and didn't get any answer. Quinn wasn't answering her phone either. He was frantic.

He spotted a police car at the elementary school where the parade ended. He met the officer halfway to his patrol car after jumping from the float after it stopped. "Has something happened, Bill," he asked after realizing who the officer was.

"There's been an incident at your house. Quinn is fine and Remy is at the hospital. She'll be okay. He wanted to reassure Archer of that right off the bat. I'll take you there but you have to stay calm. I can't handle you collapsing on me!" the officer said as Archer started to breathe heavily and look as if he would keel right over on the pavement.

Quinn saw Archer run from the police cruiser into the hospital. She ran to intercept him before he went into the emergency room.

"Wait a minute, Dad. Let's sit down and talk for a few minutes before you go rushing in to see mom all red in the face and acting like a crazy man. Believe me, she doesn't need you to have a heart attack!" Quinn led her dad over to one of the sofas in the foyer.

"I need to see her, Quinn. I have to see for myself that she's okay." Archer was panting like a race horse at the end of a race. His breathing was so heavy Quinn was getting very concerned.

"In a minute, Dad. You have got to calm down. Let your heart rate settle to a more reasonable number first. You're getting all worked up. Mom is okay. She's okay, I promise you that. She has a few bruises and a mild concussion but she is doing great. Just sit for awhile and allow me to tell you what happened." Quinn spoke softly in an attempt to keep her dad calm.

"All right, honey. Suppose you tell me just what happened today. Don't leave anything out. I will listen and get myself settled God, I am just so upset to know something happened to Remy," he cried in anguish.

"It's okay, it's okay. Try to relax and we'll sit here and we'll talk it out. By that time you will be in control and maybe it will be time to go see mom." Quinn took his hands in hers and they sat there together, father and daughter.

"I went to the house right after you called me. I went into the house and called for mom but she didn't answer and she wasn't upstairs or down. I went into the garage thinking she must be in there because her car was parked outside.

When I opened the door I saw a man with a shotgun poised at mom's head."

"Oh my God," exclaimed Archer, dropping his head to his hands. "Oh my Lord," he repeated, shaking his head.

"Stop, Dad. Now listen to me. Mom was okay, just scared. This guy motioned for me to come closer. He was the ugliest man I have ever seen. His face was grotesque, his eyes were pure evil.

I asked him, who he was and what was he doing here holding a gun to my mother's head. I was trying to remain calm so mom wouldn't panic.

Out of his mouth came a terrible laugh and he curled his lips up in a terrible snarl before answering me."

"Why honey, I'm your worst nightmare, the man who murdered your father and got away with it." Then he laughed again. "I didn't fire the killing shot. Corinne's hired goons did that. I just shot him again to make sure the son of a bitch was dead."

"You're John Farraday, aren't you?" I asked.

"You finally have the guts to show your ugly face back in Grey Falls River. Let my mother go, you loathsome pig, and take me hostage. She hasn't done a thing to you."

"He just looked at me so I spit in his face. He reached out and shoved me hard against the wall but I bounced right back in his face."

"Get in the truck," he commanded. "We're all going for a nice little ride."

I glanced at the truck and it was the same truck that hit me coming out of the library. I could see the dent in the front grill work.

"I looked at the shotgun and my eyes must have gotten really wide."

"Yep, it's the same gun, you bitch. A bit of nostalgia to be killed by the long lost murder weapon! I've been looking forward to this for a long time. Now get in the truck before I cause harm to your little momma here."

"I took a step toward him and he took his foot and kicked me hard enough that I hit the floor and slid into the wall hitting my head. My phone fell out of my pocket but he didn't see it. I made a point of slowly rising and as I turned I held my head with one hand and snapped a quick picture of him with the other and then tossed the phone away.

I told him that if he intended to kill both of us he would have to do it right here, in the garage. We weren't getting in the truck. His eyes just filled with fury and his stare penetrated the space between us. Before I could react he had swung the butt end of the shotgun and caught mom square in the face."

Archer's face reacted in such a manner, Quinn thought he was going to faint for sure. He shook his head and said in a menacing tone, "That bastard! That cowardly poor excuse for a human being! I wish I could kill him dead this very minute!"

"I know Dad, I reacted the same way. I don't even know how I remembered but I had put a screwdriver in my pocket as I left the hall. I had been helping decorate and just put it away when you called.

I was so furious I drew it out of my jacket pocket and lunged at him. He was off balance and I thrust that screwdriver full force into his neck clear up to the hilt. He got this look of amazement on his face and fell to the floor, dead."

It was silent for a moment. They both were absorbing what she had just said. Finally her dad spoke.

"You did a very brave thing. I am so proud of you. You saved your mother's life. I am so grateful." Archer began to weep as he held his daughter in his arms.

Quinn patted his back and told him it was okay. Now they could go in and see Remy and he would be composed and able to visit her quietly and not be a nervous, rambling wreck.

Remy was conscious but not able to speak coherently. Her one eye was swollen shut and turning black. Her broken nose was swollen so you could hardly tell there was a space between her eyes and her nose. She had numerous cuts and bruises from the blow to the face. She was having trouble breathing so she was on oxygen. The nurses made her comfortable and told Archer he could see her but just for a few minutes.

"My beautiful, sweet Remy," he whispered, bending down to lightly kiss her forehead. "I am so sorry, sweetheart."

"Aaar." . . . she tried to speak but he shushed her gently with his fingers on her lips.

"Ssssh, my darling. Just rest. I'm here and you're safe and in good hands." Archer took her hands in his large ones and caressed her fingers. "Just rest, I'm here and everything is okay."

Watching through the window, Quinn just broke down and wept at this tender scene. This was true love. It's what she wanted in her life. She tiptoed into the room and gave both parents a kiss. She told her dad she would come by later and left the hospital to go home and talk to the detective in charge.

The doctor had wanted her to stay overnight in case she had suffered another concussion from her hit on the head but she refused.

An officer had been assigned to accompany her so he drove her home. When they arrived at the scene there were police cars, tech vans, the coroner, and many press and media vehicles.

"Don't worry, Ms. Reaghan, I'll see you safely inside. You don't have to answer any questions out here. It's a mob scene!"

They quickly pushed their way into the house. Took came to meet her and directed her to a chair.

"Just stay here a few minutes and the chief will be here to ask you a few questions. Would you like a drink of something? How's your head? Are you okay?"

He was being so kind and understanding that Quinn just wanted to give him a hug.

"I'm fine, Took. I am just exhausted. This has been quite a day. I really don't think I can go tonight. I just feel so bad about my mom.

I caused her this pain and her terror. I am just sick about it!"

"Q," Took said. "You saved her life. Just start there and be grateful for that. Don't let the guilt take over your life. It happened and it's done. You're a hero."

"No, I'm not a hero. I reacted from pure hatred. There was nothing heroic about it."

"It's only a little after two. Let's get through this interview and see what happens. We can do this. I'll be right here beside you." Took gave her a hug and left to get her a cold drink.

Quinn retold her story and told it again until everyone was satisfied. The police had found her phone. The body hadn't been removed as yet so Quinn went upstairs to her parent's room and laid down on the bed. She knew Took would take care of everything once the body was removed and everyone left.

She should call Brick and tell him about her mother but she didn't feel quite up to that. She called the hospital and was reassured her mother was doing fine. Archer told her to try and relax and get ready for her big night.

Right, thought Quinn. Like I can really put this out of my mind and go to a dinner dance like nothing ever happened. The doctor had given her medication for her nerves so she took one and tried to relax. A few minutes later she drifted off to sleep.

A few hours later she awoke to find Penny sitting in the chair by the bed.

"Good afternoon, girlfriend," Penny said with a smile. "I brought all my clothes and stuff here so can get ready for tonight's festivities together. Just like the old days when we were going to the prom."

"Oh, Penny, I just don't think I can do this. Mom's in the hospital and I just don't feel up to putting on a smiling face and be out in public partying after all that's happened."

"Then you're letting John Farraday win, Q. Your mom is doing fine, your dad is with her for the night. You'll be here by yourself after all the time and effort you've put into this tenth reunion. Come on Q, just for a little while. If it doesn't work, I'll bring you home. Give it a try and see how it goes."

Quinn got up and walked into the bathroom and splashed some cold water on her face. She thought about what Penny had said. She supposed she could go for a little while. After all, Penny was right. She would just be here by herself. She really didn't want to be alone. Maybe being out among friends would be good for her, help her forget the day's events.

"Okay, Penny. Bring on my new dress and shoes! We are going dancing!"

"That's the spirit! Screw everybody! We are going to hold our heads high and walk in that place like we are taking over! No guilt, no self pity and no crying jags! Just a couple beautiful women on the prowl!" Penny grabbed Quinn and danced her around the room. Finally Quinn began to relax and a smile came back to her face.

"You're one crazy broad, Penny Stovall!" she said. "Tonight will either kill me or cure me. You can shower in my parent's bathroom and I'll be in mine. You are absolutely right. We'll worry about tomorrow, tomorrow!"

CHAPTER TWENTY-EIGHT

Quinn was astounded when she walked into room where the dinner dance was to take place. The room was decorated so beautifully. The ceiling was especially spectacular. Draped with gossamer from one wall to another and tiny twinkling lights shining through brought the room to life. It was like a fairy tale come true. She looked like a princess in her beautiful light blue chiffon evening gown. Her blonde hair and blue eyes were shining with happiness at seeing how lovely everything was and all her high school friends coming forward to give her hugs.

Of course there were questions from all directions. Finally, Took grabbed the microphone on the stage and told everyone to relax and let Quinn enjoy the evening.

Everyone could read all about the day's events in the morning paper.

Penny introduced the master of ceremonies for the evening and he came forward to make a few announcements. He asked everyone to take their seats and following a prayer by the class chaplain, dinner was served.

While Quinn was eating and chatting gaily with her friends, a photographer slipped into the room and began snapping pictures. Took jumped up from the table and demanded he leave immediately or face arrest.

That was not a pleasant start to her evening but she was grateful for Took taking care of the situation before it became ugly. He had plenty of the men present to back him up and the photographer quickly left without putting up any resistance.

Quinn thanked them all and was told not to worry about a thing. Her classmates had her back. Several asked her where Brick was. They were looking forward to meeting her handsome, movie star, detective, husband. Quinn apologized for him not being able to attend. She could see the disappointment in a lot of faces.

She became quiet and Penny was afraid she was falling into depression again and would want to leave. She announced a class picture would be taken before the dancing began. She asked Quinn to help direct everyone on to the platforms that had been set up for this purpose. By the time everyone was in place, Quinn was once again smiling and joking with her friends.

The band took the stage following the picture taking. While they were warming up, Quinn excused herself and went to the ladies room. When she emerged a crowd had formed around an individual who had just entered the hall. Lots of laughter was heard and the women were giggling like a bunch of school girls amid a football team practice.

When the group spotted Quinn they parted like the Red Sea. Quinn gasped and ran forward and threw her arms around her husband who was standing grinning like a kitten with a bowl of cream.

"Brick, oh Brick," she cried hugging him so hard he began to beg for release. Quinn could not believe he was actually here. How she had dreamed and wished he would come. Finally she felt safe.

"I think we have a few things to discuss," he said as he waved everyone away. They all wanted a picture with him and an autograph. "Listen, everyone," he began, "I am so glad to be here but I haven't seen my lovely wife in two months. I'd like to have her to myself for a bit. Thank you for your attention. Penny has some autographed pictures if you would like one. I hope I'm not being rude or sounding pretentious, I just really need to have some alone time with Quinn."

The band began playing *Unchained Melody* so Quinn asked if they could have this one dance. He put his arms around her and they danced with him holding her tightly against him. He looked down into her eyes and whispered, "I love you," so tenderly Quinn thought she would melt down to the floor.

When the dance ended she said her goodbyes and hugged her friends. She gave Penny and Took an extra hug and a kiss too. She would never forget their kindness and help. She told them she would be in touch before returning to San Diego.

The crowd of media was still hanging around the building. When Quinn and Brick walked out the crowd erupted with questions and were pushing microphones in their faces.

Brick was used to this type of chaos so he calmly grabbed the nearest microphone and the crowd quieted.

Brick pushed Quinn behind him as he began to speak. "Thank you for being here tonight. I realize it has been a very eventful day. If you give my wife and I a brief time alone, I promise to give you an interview tomorrow evening at six o'clock at the police station. Now if you'll excuse us, we would appreciate your courtesy and understanding."

When he handed the microphone back to the reporter, she thanked him and the crowd dispersed, letting the couple through.

Brick guided Quinn to his car and they left without incident. They didn't drive to her parent's home so Quinn had no idea where they were headed.

Brick was quiet as he drove through town and headed out to the country.

"Where are we going, Brick?" Quinn asked as she watched familiar landmarks flash by in the night.

"We are going out to the lake. To your parent's cottage. Someplace nice and quiet and private where we won't be interrupted or spied upon by the media," he replied.

Quinn hadn't been to the lake cottage for many years. When she had gone fishing with Archer that's all they did was fish. They hadn't come to the cottage. She had loved the cottage as a child. It was built with logs and had a huge wraparound porch. Inside was a large kitchen that adjoined a living area bordered on one side by a massive fireplace. There was a bathroom downstairs and a small den. There was a loft upstairs and two more bedrooms and a bath.

Quinn was surprised to see everything in working order and a cozy fire burning in the fireplace.

"Have you already been here?" she asked, looking around the room.

"Yes, I came directly here from the airport. I planned to surprise you tonight but I am the one who has been totally surprised by the day's events. We will discuss this further after I bring in your overnight bag and settle in.

With that said, Brick went out to the car. Quinn was left wondering what exactly he knew about everything that had happened.

She noticed fresh flowers sitting on the kitchen table. Brick must have brought those for me, she thought. He knew how much she loved flowers. Here he was thinking they could have a romantic hideaway and instead he walked into a hailstorm.

Brick carried the bag up to the loft before going into the kitchen and coming out with a bottle of champagne and two champagne glasses. He brought them into the living room and placed them on the table in front of the large L-shaped sofa. He motioned for Quinn to take a seat. He stood in front of the fireplace and proceeded to speak.

"I thought I would fly in and surprise you by showing up for your class reunion. You can imagine my horror at finding out what had gone on today before my arrival."

Quinn opened her mouth to say something but he raised his hand and silenced her.

"Please, let me finish. I called from the plane and no one answered at the house. I called your dad's cell phone and imagine my shock at finding him at the hospital! He called Took and he met me here when I arrived.

Now I know the whole story, at least from his point of view. I don't know whether to strangle you or love you to death. My Nancy Drew has turned into Steven Segall!"

Again Quinn attempted to speak but this time he put his finger to his lips and she became quiet once more.

"I know you must have been frightened to death, especially for your mom. I understand that. I cannot fathom why I wasn't informed about everything else that has been going on since you arrived in Grey Falls River. This has made me most unhappy.

I am relieved that Remy is going to be okay. The events have almost given Archer heart failure. Sergeant Ryder is threatening retirement from the angst you have caused in the two months you have been in town. He has begged me to take you back to California and never return to Grey Falls River."

Brick waited for her response but when she remained silent he continued his tirade.

"I am now giving you the opportunity to explain yourself. Maybe we should exchange positions. I feel I should be seated when you tell me everything that has gone on since day one." He sat down and crossed his arms and signaled for her to begin.

Quinn didn't know where to begin.

"So, Ms. Federal Prosecutor, are you at a loss for words?" Brick asked. "I find that hard to believe. Was this your intention when you panned this trip? To find the murderer of your biological father? Let's start there."

"First," Quinn stammered before collecting herself and continuing. "I am so sorry for everything that has happened. I certainly didn't plan on my mother getting hurt and almost killed. It began so simply. I visited my father's grave and it sort of developed from there. I just thought I would do a little investigating never thinking it would get so out of control." Quinn looked down at the floor before continuing. The last thing she wanted to do was to break down in front of Brick. She had to tell him her side of the story.

"Brick, there were so many suspects. You would not believe how people opened up with me when they heard I was investigating this old case. It was truly unbelievable! I had a list you would not believe. Even my own mother was a suspect. I interviewed so many people and asked so many questions. I really did not intend to put myself or anyone else in a dangerous situation. It just sort of, you know, happened." She looked at Brick like she was sure he would agree and nod his head in understanding.

Brick stood and faced her before speaking. "Did it ever occur to you that someone might not like your prying into this case? Did you ever think it could have serious repercussions? Quinn, did you ever take a minute and ask yourself, should I be doing this?" Brick shook his head in disbelief. "You are not a trained police officer. You are an attorney. You try cases in court. You do not solve them. You do not carry a gun, a badge or paperwork that gives you the right to be judge and jury. You could have been killed! Your mother could have been killed and you would have been responsible! I am furious with you!"

Quinn looked him square in the eye. "I know you are angry with me. You have every right to be. I am not happy with myself. I let things get out of hand. I admit that. But, I had to keep trying. I knew the Grey Falls River Police Department did not handle the case the way it should have been handled. Brick, they never allowed any outside law enforcement agencies to help in their investigation. The police chief actually refused to use the State Police Lab.

He said the police department could handle it alone. What a joke. The chief was a joke. He was not respected by his own men. He knew nothing about investigating a murder."

Brick sat back down quietly and told her to continue.

"Look at the list of suspects, Brick. The ex-husband of Quade's girlfriend, the son of Quade's wife, the best friend of the wife, the chief of police, the girlfriend of Quade, my own mother, or an unknown. Okay, the girlfriend of the wife is dead. Even so, she was a woman and I can't believe she could have shot him twice. I borrowed my dad's shotgun and I was knocked on my butt when I shot it. Plus, think about it. Commit murder for a friend? That's asking a lot. Risk life in prison or the death sentence for a friend? I doubt it. The son wasn't close to Quade. No one has said he hated Quade or wished him dead. My mother? How ludicrous is that? She loved him.

His wife? There again, he was a big strong guy. Shoot him twice? Where was the weapon?

How did she shoot him twice, dispose of the gun and stagger outside, become incoherent and disoriented and collapse? The police chief? Yes, he had access to a shotgun. Yes, he'd been dating Corinne. He and Quade had a fight two days before the murder and Quade had beaten the crap out of him. What man wouldn't want revenge for that? It's perfect. The police department's shotgun. Who would check it even if it had been found at the department days later? No outside law enforcement to double check the evidence. The police chief retiring in a few months and leaving the state, the case not solved. It was too crazy to not pursue it. I couldn't just let it go."

Quinn sat down on the hearth and held her head in her hands.

"Okay Quinn, let's stop for now. We both need to relax and get our minds off this tonight. You're exhausted. Let's have a glass of champagne and drink to a better day tomorrow."

215

They finished off the entire bottle of champagne while sitting quietly and talking softly about the reunion and other fun things she had done. As they talked they drew closer together. Finally, Brick drew her close beside him and caressed her face and the back of her neck.

"Quinn, you know I love you and I know that you love me. This series of incidents has taught us both that life is tenuous. Our arrangement is ridiculous. It's time we decide where this marriage is going."

They sat for a minute, neither of them speaking. Both sat staring into the fire. The silence was welcome. It became a serious moment, each deciding where to start to begin a new commitment to each other.

They turned to look at each other at the same time. They looked into each other's eyes and their heads drew closer together. The kiss they shared seemed to go on forever. For a moment the world ceased to exist for two people who had rediscovered love.

Brick led her to the bedroom. Slowly he undressed her piece by piece of clothing, kissing the place where each garment had bared her skin. Quinn unbuttoned his shirt and slid it off his shoulders and unbuckled his belt, kissing every square inch of his body.

They fell on to the bed clutching each other in a moment of unbridled passion.

No words were exchanged, just the moans and groans and sighs released by spent bodies in the throes of ecstasy coming together with a need that overpowers the mind.

The night was spent fulfilling the hunger that had erupted in two souls who never should have been apart.

It was as if they couldn't satisfy some primal need. By morning they were both in a much needed deep sleep. It was noon before they awakened. Brick wanted to stay there forever, just loving his bride.

Quinn was content to just lie there in her husband's arms. Their night together was glorious. The lovemaking was the best ever.

She was so in love with her husband that she thought her heart would surely explode.

Eventually they knew they had to get up and begin their day. Quinn found some clothes she had left there in her teens. The jeans were tight in some places but Brick didn't seem to mind. She took a top from her mother's closet so at least she didn't have to go back to town in her evening gown.

Brick had the necessities so they were all set. He looked comfortable in jeans and a tee shirt.

"Let's go into town and get a bite to eat," he said as she came down the stairs and walked right into his arms. "You are beautiful this morning, woman. You look like you've been well loved."

Quinn wrapped her arms around his neck and drew his face down to hers. She kissed him long and hard and he almost led them back up to the bedroom.

"Come on, lover boy," Quinn said dreamily. "We have to get back to reality sometime. Mom comes home today, I think. We have to make sure the garage is cleaned up and there's no evidence of the events of yesterday. I don't want her freaking out."

"Okay, Nancy Drew," Brick responded, leading her out the door. As he opened the car door for her he gave her a swat on her backside as she entered the vehicle. "That's for later, when you need it," he said, laughing. "And I know you will be needing it!"

When they drove into the driveway they noticed the house was in good shape. The garage doors were down and her mother's car was parked in the driveway.

When they unlocked the front door and entered the house, everything was neatly in place.

The garage had been cleaned and everything looked like normal.

"That's what friends do for friends," a voice said behind them.

It was her parent's neighbors from next door and across the street.

"We got together and decided we would take care of everything after the police cleared the property from their investigation," said Bob Hedges, a close friend and neighbor for years.

'Thank you so much," so Quinn. "We can't ever repay you for your kindness. It's a wonderful thing that you have done. My mother will be so grateful."

After the neighbors had left, the couple called the hospital to check on Remy. Archer told them she would be released in a little bit and he would be bringing Remy home. All the children would be stopping by to see her but they promised they wouldn't stay long and tire her out. He said they would just order in pizza and keep it light.

CHAPTER TWENTY-NINE

Quinn was supposed to return to San Diego the following morning. There were still some things to be taken care of so she called her boss and told him the circumstances so he gave her an extra week to wrap things up.

Brick was supposed to fly with her but he said he wasn't going anywhere without her by his side.

Quinn was called into the police station to answer some more questions about the case. The police chief wanted to know how John Farraday knew she was in Grey Falls River investigating the cold case.

Quinn told him she wondered about that herself. She had a feeling someone in Grey Falls River had called him and told him what was going on. She had her suspicions who it was but she didn't want to accuse anyone without proof. She only said it might be beneficial to check the cell phone records of the man in charge of the newspaper.

The case was declared closed. The two hired thugs would never be found. Quinn never revealed what Hank Kidder had told her. He was a broken man and nothing would be gained by putting him on trial. It wouldn't bring her father back and it would destroy a family.

After they left the police station, Brick drove Quinn to the cemetery so they could pay their final respects to Quade Mervin Reaghan. As they were sitting on a bench near the grave, Brick told Quinn he thought this would be the perfect setting for him to tell her his version of what went down with her biological father on that fateful day twenty-eight years ago.

"You did a very good job, Quinn, and I am proud of you even though it could have been a disaster.

I agree with you that this was a simple crime that should have been solved in short order. It was a crime of passion. It involved amateurs for the most part. The killer may have been a thug and possibly he could have committed other murders. That we will never know.

Corinne was a woman who was full of hate and wanted revenge because the man she loved was in love with another woman. She had never killed anyone or had never witnessed a murder. You cannot imagine the horror of seeing a person killed in front of your eyes for the first time.

I am sure that is why she began screaming and almost lost her mind. A normal human being, not a trained assassin, would be overcome with emotion. If they were directly responsible for the death of another person, especially a loved one, the guilt would be tremendous.

Hank Kidder told you that Corinne had hired a couple of men she had met at this disreputable bar to carry out her plan to kill Quade. Farraday confirmed that to you. One was going to pretend to be a realtor there to see the house and the other was to be hiding in the basement waiting for Quade to come down the stairs and turn to the left and he would shoot him in the back with a shotgun. That was the plan. This weapon was never found until the other day.

Now then, no one saw a strange car in the driveway. The neighbor said he remembered just seeing Quade's truck. Corinne's car was found two days after the murder parked on a side street in a town about fifteen miles away from Grey Falls River.

How did the killers get to the house and where was their vehicle? How did Corinne's van get to the next town? If Farraday was there, where was his car? No one reported seeing a police cruiser parked at the house.

The golf course backed up to Quade's house. The drive into the golf course was right next to their house.

I am sure the police at least looked for footprints leading from the house across the yard.

I don't understand why there were no fingerprints on the railing leading down the stairs. A realtor wouldn't keep his gloves on in the house.

Following the shooting, I imagine the two thugs took off immediately. Farraday was busy dealing with a hysterical Corinne Reaghan. He roughed her up a bit and then he took off. Did he have time to wipe away any fingerprints from the scene?

Corinne's car was clean as a whistle the police report stated. If Farraday had driven the car he would have made sure of that.

I think Corinne drove to the town, met the two men she had hired, rode with them to the golf course where they parked their car, went inside the house and she called Quade. Her plan was to ride back to the town with them, pick up her van and drive home, find the body and call the police.

Farraday could have driven his personal car to the golf course, walked down the driveway, leaving no footprints, into the driveway at

Quade's, into the garage and down to the basement.

I can't explain why there wasn't public outcry when no outside agency was helping and nothing seemed to be done to solve this simple crime. I am sure John Farraday was having many a sleepless night worrying about what Corinne might say or confess.

It amazes me that Corinne wasn't killed the same night as Quade. What made the difference? Maybe the two hired men hadn't been paid their money. Maybe Corinne was making too much racket after the killing that everyone just got the hell out of there thinking someone must have heard all her screaming.

John Farraday planned his move well. He killed Corinne and made it look like a suicide. I think he was afraid he had made too many mistakes and too many people were asking too many questions.

He was just a normal man who tried to commit a serious crime without knowing how to get away with it.

He would have gotten away with it if it weren't for Quade's daughter showing up twenty-eight years later and asking questions. You weren't even born when it happened and yet you solved the case.

Truly the grave yields answers. Even Farraday's efforts to frighten and stop you were amateurish. He was so intimidated by your investigation that he blindly and stupidly acted on impulse and blundered his way to his guilt and subsequent death."

"Wow, that's quite a story, Brick. Does Took know all of this?"

"Yes, we talked quite extensively about the case the day I arrived and again since then. We both wondered if Farraday took the two hired killers out the same night. Anything is possible. Being the chief of police he could have covered up everything. They were witnesses and could identify him. If they weren't paid the money, they would certainly come back for it at some point. If they were paid, Farraday could have killed them and kept the money himself. There are many scenarios and we will never have all the answers on this one."

He took Quinn's hand and helped her to her feet. "Let's say our final goodbye and hope the Good Lord blesses his soul one more time."

Quinn knelt down and patted his stone for the last time. "Goodbye, Daddy. Rest in peace. I love you."

CHAPTER THIRTY

Remy was getting stronger and would soon be back to normal. Archer said they would be taking a cruise to heal her body and her spirit. Remy laughed at that but said she was looking forward to lying on the deck and being waited on hand and foot and not cooking!

Brick and Quinn decided that it would be a perfect time to renew their wedding vows while they were there with Quinn's family. It was going to be held at the lake cottage the following weekend. Brick notified his parents and they were so excited they promised to fly there to be at the ceremony.

Emily said she would bake the cake. Carrie wanted to take care of the catering. Remy asked if she and Archer could finally give their daughter away. They were not at their first wedding so they were thrilled to host this wonderful event.

Archer's and Remy's pastor was going to officiate.

Quinn decided she would wear the same dress she wore to the class reunion. She wanted to show it off as she hadn't worn it very long! Luckily, Brick had his suit he had worn to the reunion.

Gramma Annie wanted a new dress for the occasion so Remy and Quinn took her shopping a few days before the grand event. She was so happy she even insisted on buying a new hat.

The big day arrived and the weather was perfect. Blue skies and sunshine welcomed the guests arriving for the ceremony. Chairs had been set up down by the lake on the expansive lawn. Archer had found an old gazebo in the shed. He repainted it a sparkling white and Remy had the florist in town cover it with fresh ivy.

Brick's parents arrived just as the minister drove into the driveway. Introductions were made and once everyone was seated, the renewal of vows began.

Brick stood at the center of the gazebo by the pastor. A friend of Penny's sang *Wind Beneath My Wings* which made the tears begin to flow.

Everyone stood as the door to the cottage opened and Quinn stepped out with a parent on either side and began her walk down to her beloved Brick. He couldn't wait that long so he began walking toward her and they met in the middle and shared a long kiss. Everyone shouted it was too soon to do that!

Brick and Quinn just smiled and continued their walk until they were at the gazebo.

The renewal of vows was said with each of them promising a renewal of their commitment to each other and then Brick spoke of his love for her and she expressed her love for him.

It was a very moving moment. There was a beautiful silence. Then everyone cheered and began to congratulate the couple and talk all at once.

Archer had a band playing up at the cottage and a dance floor had been set up in the driveway. The food was served inside. Tables had been set up on the lawn and on the porch.

The family and friends were all having a terrific time. Jack and Jane Rainwater were so delighted to meet everyone and be there they promised to come back every year.

Brick and Quinn stayed until the very end. They were spending the night at the cottage. They were thrilled everyone had come. It was extra special because their first wedding had been just them and a few witnesses.

The beginning and the end of the two-month vacation Quinn had planned on were very different. She was thinking she had dreamed the whole thing. It was so unimaginable.

Brick carried her up to the bedroom and laid her down on a coverlet covered with red rose petals. A new, lovely white peignoir set was lying on the pillow. It was beautiful but

Brick told her she wouldn't be needing that tonight.

Soft music was playing and the room was filled with the sweet scent of a flower garden in the spring.

The window was open and the sound of crickets and frogs and the waves slapping against the shore made for a beautiful chorus.

No words were needed or spoken as the couple came together in a new way, in a new life. Friends, lovers, and husband and wife.

CHAPTER THIRTY-ONE

Quinn and Brick visited Took and Janis to say goodbye. Penny and her new fiance', Steve, came over with their two children. The three couples enjoyed a barbecue and promised each other they would always remain good friends.

Took said he supposed Quinn could return to Grey Falls River but only if Brick came with her.

Brick invited everyone to visit them in California. He said he would take them all, even the children, he said with a wink at their parents, to Disneyland.

The kids all whooped and hollered over that and asked their parents if they could go home and pack right now.

The next morning Brick and Quinn thanked Remy and Archer, kissed and hugged them goodbye and told them to come for a visit soon.

The couple had a lot of time to discuss their future plans on the way to the airport and then the flight to San Diego.

They decided Quinn would go home first and get back to her job. Brick would stay at her place a few days getting things together and then he would go back to Los Angeles and back to his job.

They decided to look for a house in between the two cities. Both could commute by train.

That plan fell through when Quinn discovered she was pregnant a month after their return home. The happy couple then went house hunting nearer Los Angeles. Quinn would be staying home for a few years. If she wanted to continue her career at that time as a federal prosecutor she would transfer to Los Angeles.

Eight months later she delivered a healthy baby boy who they named, Jack Archer Reaghan Rainwater.

Both sets of grandparents were present for the christening. A rainbow appeared in the sky as they were leaving the chapel overlooking the Pacific Ocean.

Quinn and Brick whispered a silent prayer of thanks for the blessing they had just received.

THE END

CPSIA information can be obtained at www.ICGtesting.com
Printed in the USA
BVOW032310041112

304480BV00006B/1/P